His eyes were too obscured in shadow for me to see their magic, but I knew it was there

I could feel his searing gaze better than I could see it. This thing that was passing between us was no longer ambiguous. My heart yearned for him . . . and raced with fear.

He drew me slowly toward him, his grip so firm, it almost hurt as he crushed me against him. He covered my mouth and I kissed him back, as hard as he kissed me. My body throbbed and my desire was suddenly insatiable.

The next thing I knew he'd lifted me into his arms, without our mouths even parting. When he began carrying me toward the stairway, the kiss finally ended.

And in my heart of hearts, I knew that *this* was what I'd wanted from the first time I'd laid eyes on him.

Dear Reader,

How many times a day have you heard the phrase, "Guess what happened to me"? We all tell stories to live. All day long, our friends and families tell us their stories—confiding in us all their secret joys and sorrows.

That's exactly what Janice Kaiser's heroines do in *Betrayal* and *Deceptions* (November 1993), our latest "Editor's Choice" selections. In these stories, you will meet two remarkable women, Allison Stephens and Darcy Hunter, who will confide all their secrets, all their moments of joy and sorrow in their own distinctive, unforgettable voices.

We, the editors, believe that the emotional power, the intensity and intimacy of these voices and these books will appeal to you as much as they did to us.

Once you start listening to Allison's and Darcy's voices, you'll be enthralled and moved. Their stories will forever be in your hearts and imaginations. We'd love to hear how you like these books.

The Editors
Harlequin Temptation
225 Duncan Mill Road
Don Mills, Ontario, Canada
M3B 3K9

BETRAYAL
JANICE KAISER

Harlequin Books

TORONTO • NEW YORK • LONDON
AMSTERDAM • PARIS • SYDNEY • HAMBURG
STOCKHOLM • ATHENS • TOKYO • MILAN
MADRID • WARSAW • BUDAPEST • AUCKLAND

For Sherie Posesorski,
who, with her skill and imagination,
helps turn dreams into novels.

Published October 1993

ISBN 0-373-25562-4

BETRAYAL

1

THEY SAY THAT EVERYTHING happens for a reason. And yet, when Gloria came to my apartment one night to ask a favor, I never would have guessed that my safe, settled, predictable life would be changed forever. But it was.

Gloria ran a design firm and I worked for her free-lance as a commercial artist. Even though we were completely different—both in looks and personality—we'd become close friends. Gloria was outgoing, confident, virtually fearless—determined to make the most of life's opportunities, whatever the cost. And though she took great pleasure from her work and friends, men were the meat and potatoes of her existence.

I, on the other hand, was contained, reserved, cautious. Men were not a big part of my life. And I had learned to find contentment, if not happiness, in my solitude. Perhaps that was why Gloria had once asked whether my imagination didn't seethe with secret passions, if I didn't dream about some marvelous man coming into my life. I was embarrassed by the question because I never spoke of such things to anyone, not even to her.

It was about a month before that fateful night that Gloria first told me of her plan to vacation at a resort in Mexico that catered to singles. "Why don't you come with me, Allison?" she'd pleaded. "How long has it been since you've been away, since you just went someplace to have fun?"

"I don't know. A long time," I admitted. The truth was, I had never gone on that sort of vacation. It wasn't that I was a prude, it just wasn't me. And in her heart, I think Gloria understood that.

Yet in the days before she was scheduled to leave, I often found myself wondering about the choices I had made. A part of me longed to be more adventurous, though I couldn't seem to find the will to make things happen. It was as if I was waiting for the world—for my future—to come to me.

And then on that foggy night in mid-October, fate did come to my front door, right along with Gloria. She looked thoroughly exhausted. "I think you're ready for this vacation," I said, noticing her drawn face and slumped shoulders.

"I won't even be going unless you do me a big, big favor, Allison," she replied.

She was lugging the portfolio we used to transport drawings and plates between her shop and my apartment, where I'd set up a studio. Though somewhat unorthodox, the arrangement worked for us. I was able to earn a comfortable living without having to worry about administrative details or dealing with the public. Gloria took care of all that.

"What sort of favor?" I asked.

She plopped down in the worn dark green armchair I'd had since college and looked at me, the moisture from the fog still glistening in her hair. "You know the design package you did for ComTech last week?"

"Yes?"

"Well, David Higson, the owner, wants to finalize everything at once. We weren't supposed to have it ready until the end of the month, but he needs it now . . . something about refinancing his company. Anyway, he has to have his new corporate logo right away, which means camera-ready art to the printer this week."

"Oh, no."

"Right," Gloria said. "Either I cancel Mexico and deal with him tomorrow morning, or I get on my plane and you meet him in my place."

"Me?" My heart dropped right into my stomach.

"I wouldn't ask, Allison, but since you'd be making the changes anyway, I thought it would be just as well if you spoke with him directly."

"You know how bad I am at that sort of thing," I groaned.

"You don't have to sell him anything. Just listen to what he wants. You can handle that."

I could, of course. Gloria was right. I wouldn't be called on to play all those manipulative games businessmen love so much. But the thought of having to deal with someone who was annoyed or under pressure did not sit well with me. I hated those kinds of situations.

"If it's all right, I'll leave the art and drawings with you now," Gloria said. "Take them to the shop in the morning and Mr. Higson will meet you there at nine. He's actually a pretty nice guy."

"All right," I said, looking at the case. "I'll do my best."

Gloria smiled. "I wouldn't ask," she said, "but Com-Tech is my first Silicon Valley account, and I'd really like to please them. People down there are really thick. Besides, you don't have to charm him or anything. Just let a little of that natural sweetness of yours come through."

I bit my lip. Gloria got up and gave me a reassuring hug. "This isn't your thing, I know," she said. "But it's good for you to do something like this every once in a while. And damn it, you really ought to learn to deal with men. This is as good a time as any."

Gloria knew how dreadfully shy I was. It was difficult for me to face strangers, especially men. In school, I'd always been loath to speak in class. And as an adult I'd become adept at avoiding situations I couldn't handle.

"It's not good for you to stay cooped up in here for days on end, slaving over your drafting table," Gloria said. "I'd go nuts without some interaction with people."

I'd heard that speech before, but I smiled at her motherly goading anyway. "Don't worry. I'll meet with Mr. Higson and you can go to Mexico," I assured her.

I wasn't really a hermit, though Gloria thought so. I spent a lot of time among people—though anonymously, among strangers. I walked a lot. I loved Golden Gate Park. I spent hours in the museums and galleries, my sketchbook in hand. I'd spent whole days with the Rodin collection in the California Palace of the Legion of Honor; I'd prowled the funky shops on Clement Street, the coffee houses on Union; and I loved the downtown department stores at Christmas—the crowds, the bustle. I liked observing people, imagining what their lives were like.

But I knew that meeting with Mr. Higson would be a different kettle of fish altogether. He represented all sorts of potential dangers. What if he was displeased with the design package? What if he complained? What if he made demands?

The solution was easy enough, of course. I would refer him to Gloria. But the fear of something going wrong haunted me. I would have done the ComTech project for nothing or given it up altogether, rather than have to face this man and his critical eye.

Gloria went to the door. She seemed reluctant to leave, and perhaps she felt a little guilty. "I'm a rat to do this to you, aren't I?" she said.

"No, of course not."

"He's not a bad guy, Allison. Really. I mean, he's not gruff or pushy or anything like that."

"It'll be fine."

"Maybe you'll even like him. Who knows?" she said hopefully. There was a twinkle in her eye, but Gloria's mind always worked that way. It was her life's ambition to find someone for me, though she worked so hard at finding someone for herself, God knows how she found the energy to devote to my love life.

I gave her a farewell hug. "Have a wonderful trip. And don't catch anything."

She gave me one of her looks. "You mean from the water or the men?"

I flushed, which made her laugh, and she sailed off on her adventure, leaving me to face the president of ComTech. After she'd gone I leaned against the door. My heart was pounding and I felt like a complete fool. Gloria was right. I'd been in a shell too long. I was thirty-six, and here I was, acting worse than a kid. Maybe the time had come for me to rethink my life.

I wasn't bitter or disillusioned, but I'd reached the point where the disadvantages of relationships outweighed the benefits. The only man I'd ever truly cared for was one I dated during my senior year at the University of San Francisco.

Brandon and I had fallen in love sitting on the lawn behind the old Gothic stone library up on the Lone Mountain campus. We spent a lot of time together, sometimes studying, sometimes staring dreamily at the mists blanketing the hilltops of the city. We'd shared long walks in Golden Gate Park; we'd watched old movies and eaten late-night pizzas in his cramped little studio on Stanyan Street. Brandon read me poetry, he wrote poems for me.

He loved my drawings and paintings, and would gaze at them, and at me, by the hour.

I had assumed that would be enough to carry us into a life after college, but it wasn't. When he drifted off to graduate school back East, I was left in shock. I had given my love to him, and in my naive way I feared there was nothing left to give anyone else.

Brandon hadn't been the love of my life, but for a long time afterward I used my disappointment to avoid other relationships. I'd hidden behind my pain. And even though there had been two or three men after Brandon, I never truly gave of myself.

The last straw had been my affair with another artist. I'd just turned thirty, and I'd hoped Paul would prove to be my soul mate. As it turned out, he'd used me to make another woman jealous. I felt so violated, so betrayed, that I became pretty well soured on romance.

Gloria and I rarely spoke about how I'd shut men out of my life, though she had asked once whether men ever came on to me. I answered that except for someone making a casual remark to me in a bookstore or on the bus, men pretty much left me alone.

That conversation had taken place over Muu Shi pork in our favorite Chinese restaurant. We'd each had a beer. I guess my inhibitions had been lowered a bit because I'd responded with more frankness than usual. "I think men know," I said. "I think they can tell if you're truly interested, and they sense I'm not."

"They must pick up some kind of subliminal message," Gloria replied over the rim of her glass. "After all, you're better looking than I am, and men do notice me."

I suppose she intended a compliment. I was tall and very slender, unlike Gloria, who was short and a trifle pudgy. But she was also voluptuous and always did a good job with her hair and face. Still, even if Gloria was trying to be encouraging, I suspected that at some level she was pitying me, and that hurt.

"If you'd only use a little makeup and wear clothes that were more flattering," she went on, "I bet you'd be astonished by the attention you'd get."

"I'm not sure I'd know what to do with it," I answered honestly. Gloria laughed, but at the same time I knew she felt sorry for me.

And now, to do her a favor, I found myself facing the kind of situation I dreaded most. But I'd promised. She'd already left and there was no going back on my word. So I reviewed the design package, hoping to anticipate any objections Mr. Higson might have. I was sure he wouldn't like it, that he would find fault or be difficult.

I slept badly, awakening just before dawn. I didn't want to get out of bed, but I couldn't let Gloria down. My first step was to decide what to wear. It was at that moment that I began thinking of David Higson as a man, and realized he would be judging me as a woman.

My usual attire was jeans and a baggy sweater or a T-shirt. There were two dresses in my closet, but both were out of style. I had a navy linen suit I'd gotten on sale two years earlier to wear to testify in a lawsuit Gloria had brought against another design firm. As it turned out, the lawyers settled before the case went to trial. I was grateful for having been spared the ordeal of testifying, but I was stuck with the suit.

Gloria liked suits and usually wore one when she met with clients, so I decided I would wear mine. Sitting at my drafting table, or trudging through the De Young Museum in a bulky sweater and a pair of cords, I didn't have to wear makeup, but I knew I'd look like death warmed over in a suit without some lipstick, a little mascara and some blusher.

After my shower I poked through my cosmetics, resigned to disguising my usual self by pinning up my heavy reddish-gold hair and wearing makeup.

I tried to convince myself that I was merely a stand-in for Gloria, but in the back of my mind I was remembering her comments about David Higson. I recalled her innuendos, her hopes for me. And a part of me wondered if something exciting might not happen; if this wouldn't be the day that would change my life forever.

GLORIA'S SHOP WAS IN a modern brick low-rise off Chestnut, between Telegraph Hill and the waterfront. The area was filled with architectural firms, developers, investment companies. It wasn't the financial district, but there was a distinctive up-and-coming feel to the neighborhood. The rent was higher than Gloria could easily afford, but the image of the place appealed to her.

On my way there in the taxi, I wondered if my businesswoman image would fool David Higson. Somehow, I didn't think so. Even though I'd psyched myself up to act differently, underneath I knew I hadn't changed. I was still me.

I arrived fifteen minutes early. Gloria's secretary, Karen, had already made coffee. I could smell it the moment I walked in the door. She offered to fetch me a cup, but I insisted I could get it myself. She'd done a subtle double take when I'd walked in, apparently startled to see me in something other than jeans. When she told me I looked great, I was flattered.

Gloria kept the reception area filled with plants—robust ficus trees that rose to the arched ceiling, potted palms and even philodendrons. From the small supply room in back, where the coffee machine was, I could look through the forest and see Karen and the entry to the office.

I envied her easy confidence and wished I could be more like that. I glanced down at my suit, worried that it was obvious I was a fraud, and anxious whether David Higson would question my competence.

As I sipped my coffee, the president of ComTech came in the door. He was in a navy suit, the same shade as mine, and he was hesitant, as shy people in strange places so often are. I noticed that right away—the apology in his manner, the quiet discomfort with the normal courtesies. And I felt a bond with him.

He was in his mid-forties, tall, with dark, neatly trimmed hair. He had the angular, soulful face of a college professor. As he gave Karen his name, I suddenly realized Gloria's leather case was still sitting on my old green armchair at home. I had been so focused on presenting myself as a businesswoman that I'd forgotten it!

I was mortified. I withdrew deeper into the supply room, as though hiding might somehow protect me from my own ineptitude. I desperately looked around, feeling trapped. If there had been another way out, I would have left—and run all the way home.

Karen called me several times. I didn't answer. I was too paralyzed. Finally she came into the supply room.

"Mr. Higson is here, Allison," Karen said in her soft, whispery voice.

"I can't see him," I blurted out.

She blinked. "Why not? Are you sick?"

I closed my eyes and muttered, "I just can't see him, that's all."

She was at a dead loss. "Well, what should I tell him?"

"I don't know," I whispered.

Karen hesitated a moment longer, then left, closing the door behind her. I don't know what I expected—that the man would leave, that I could find a way to escape? All that mattered was that it be over. When the door opened a minute later I assumed it was Karen with an update, but it was David Higson.

"Are you all right?" he asked.

I looked into his eyes, terrified. Yet in the next instant I saw his concern. The situation suddenly seemed so absurd. I began laughing nervously, even as tears of embarrassment rolled down my cheeks.

David Higson looked totally perplexed. And the more helpless he appeared, the harder I laughed and cried. But it must have been cathartic, because after a few moments a strange calm settled over me. I wiped my nose with the back of my hand, all the while staring into his soft brown eyes.

"I'm afraid I've done something very stupid, Mr. Higson," I began. "I forgot the design package and your plates. I left them at home." It was amazing how good it felt to get it out.

"Are you serious?" he asked.

"Yes," I said, with a little burst of nervous laughter. "I forgot them."

He stared at me, apparently not knowing what to say.

"I'm sorry," I went on. "I was so anxious to be on time that when the taxi came, I just ran out the door and left everything on a chair."

He smiled, more with compassion than real amusement. "I've done the same thing myself," he said. "Half the time I go to the theater, I forget the tickets."

"Do you really?"

He nodded, looking embarrassed for me and, vicariously, for himself. The generosity of his response made me feel better.

"I'll get the package and bring it to you," I volunteered. "Where's ComTech located?"

"In Santa Clara, I'm afraid. I'm not going back there today. After finishing here, I have a meeting with my bankers and then I was planning to head for home. I'd intended to spend the day there."

"Where do you live?"

"In Richmond, just a block from the park, on 20th."

"Oh, I'm on Irving Street, near 17th."

"We're practically neighbors," he said with a hint of delight. David looked into my eyes in a shy, inquiring sort of way, and I suddenly understood why I'd dressed with such care. Everything had been leading up to this moment. And now that he'd seen me, I could tell similar thoughts were going through his mind, as well. I sensed it.

"Did you say you took a taxi here?" he asked.

"Yes. And I can take one back, collect the design package and be at your house by the time you've finished your meeting."

"Well," he said hesitantly, "since we're headed in the same direction, why don't I give you a lift? It would mean stopping off with me at the bank, but the meeting should be brief."

"Are you sure you wouldn't mind?" I asked.

"Not if you don't."

I sniffled and smiled sheepishly. David handed me his handkerchief. It was a small gesture, but it struck me as so gallant. I was usually so reserved that the smallest things affected me.

David was so like me—shy and sensitive to the feelings of others—that I felt an immediate kinship with him. And though he made me nervous, he didn't really frighten me. For the first time since Brandon, I'd felt a strong connection with a man.

For David Higson did not compel or demand, he simply offered the opportunity to share. And I felt that in him I had found the other half of me; the man for whom I was afraid to admit, even to myself, I'd been searching.

2

I DIDN'T GLANCE AT DAVID once during the drive to the Bank of America building. Even so, I was terribly aware of him. It was not his looks or any sort of physical attraction; it was the fact that he cared. I felt different around him, so alive and in tune with what was happening.

David talked a great deal, though I hardly know what about. Quite clearly, his overriding objective was to put me at ease. I sensed—actually knew right then—that he liked me. Still, the skeptic in me wondered why. Had he been taken in by my image—the makeup and the clothes? I hoped not, because I wanted it to be me he cared about, not the businesswoman I'd created.

As we walked from the parking garage to the first set of elevators, David explained that he had obtained a large loan from the bank in anticipation of a public offering of ComTech's stock. His business was at a pivotal point, and the coming weeks would be critical for both him and his partner.

I understood little of what he was saying, though I heard both hope and fear in his voice. Mainly, I was surprised how open he was with me. Perhaps he felt that since I'd exposed myself to him, he could reveal some of his worries to me.

We sat together in the reception area. David continued to talk, reaching out to me. I wanted to do the same, yet I held back, playing the good listener.

David sat with his hands on his knees. I stared at his long slim fingers and the dark hairs on the backs of his hands. He wore no rings. Until then, it hadn't occurred to me to question whether he was married. I assumed he wasn't, but I couldn't let another minute pass without knowing for sure.

"Are you married, Mr. Higson?" I asked abruptly, cutting him off in midsentence.

David was so taken aback that for a moment he didn't respond. The stock offerings or interest rates or whatever it was he'd been going on about were instantly abandoned. He looked into my eyes and said, "No. No, I'm not."

I wasn't sure if I should believe him or not. "You aren't?" I said incredulously.

"No. I'm forty-four years old and I've never been married. Sometimes it weighs on me," he admitted.

"Why?"

"People have expectations. I do for myself, so I know what it's like," he explained. "I'm not against marriage, though. It's been a matter of not finding the right person."

I was uncertain what to say next. The way he looked at me was a bit scary. David seemed sincere; I wanted to believe him. Yet I was afraid to hope this wasn't leading toward another big disappointment.

"Are *you* married?" he asked, when I sat there mutely.

I shook my head. "No."

"Divorced?"

Again I shook my head.

"Then we have something in common."

"I guess we do." I found the courage to look at him again, my hope rising as I found myself caught up in an exhilarating new emotion.

"Did it concern you that I might be married?" he asked.

If he was bold enough to ask the question, I thought I ought to be courageous enough to answer it truthfully. "Yes."

"I admire your honesty," he said.

I grew very quiet and self-conscious.

David shifted uneasily. "Can I be direct, Allison?" he finally said. "I've been trying to decide how I might invite you to lunch."

I smiled at his words—beamed, actually. It wasn't that I was eager for an invitation so much as I was relieved. My fears had been misplaced. Still, my instincts cautioned me to keep things in perspective. "What about the design package?"

"Oh, we'll take care of that, don't worry. I really do need everything this week. It would be pleasant though if we were to have lunch afterward," he said. "I wanted to express my gratitude."

His earnestness was appealing. I liked the things he said. Before we could conclude our conversation, the banker came out into the reception area and summoned David.

I was left alone in this tallest of all buildings in the city. An enormous wall of glass at the far side of the room afforded a panoramic view. I went over and peered out the window at the cars creeping over the bridge spanning the dull gray water of the bay.

Life was proceeding as usual, but not for me. Something important had happened that morning. I felt it very clearly. David Higson had affected me but, exciting as our encounter had been, I sensed he was only the catalyst. There had been a definite change. And the change was in me.

"YOU ARE A GOOD-LUCK charm, Allison," he said as we left the bank. "We were in need of an important concession, and I got it."

I glanced at David, seeing he was genuinely pleased, almost buoyant. "I'm happy for you," I said.

"Maybe it's an omen of things to come."

We got into his car and began the drive out to the western part of the city. We went over Nob Hill, then out through Pacific Heights. As we were going past Children's Hospital, David asked about my work, my life. I have never found it easy to talk about myself, but somehow I sensed it was important to share something of myself with this man.

"I live simply," I said. "I enjoy what I do. My hobby is art, so it makes up most of my life."

David Higson thought for a moment, then said, "Funny how a person's work defines who they are and how they live, isn't it?"

"Yes."

"And your career determines who you associate with, even who your friends are."

"Yet there's more to life than that," I said. "Much as I like my work, I know it's not enough."

David listened carefully, looking a little sad. "You're right, Allison, but when you've been putting the job ahead of everything else as long as I have, it becomes automatic."

"It's easy to fall into habits."

"Some things you pick up in childhood and never let go." He had a look in his eye when he said that, making me wonder whether his early years had been as difficult as mine. "How was your life as a kid?" he asked then, shifting the focus of the conversation back to me.

I told him that I'd practically been born an orphan, my mother having died in childbirth, and my father having placed me in a foster home. Then he died just as I began high school—I had hardly known him at all.

Because my father was Catholic, I was given an education at a Catholic high school and won a scholarship to the University of San Francisco. That should have made me religious, I told David, but it didn't, particularly. "I learned how to be self-reliant, though."

"Self-reliance isn't all that it's cracked up to be," he said. "I used to guard my independence jealously, but I'm not sure now that's the right way to be."

"But a person has to be able to count on him- or herself—women especially. We're vulnerable that way."

We were stopped at a traffic light. David looked over at me. "You're an attractive woman," he said. "How is it you haven't married?"

"Probably the same reason you haven't," I replied impulsively.

"I guess the standards shouldn't be any different, but it doesn't seem to fit you."

"You have to be looking for someone," I said, trying a bit harder to explain, "or at least making yourself available. And I haven't been."

"Why not?"

I suddenly realized my candor had taken me down a dangerous path. "Maybe we should talk about something else, David. If you don't mind."

He apologized unnecessarily. I felt silly, yet at the same time I was glad we'd been able to talk so directly. Rarely had I been able to speak my mind around men. My shyness was a large part of it, but lack of rapport was just as big a factor.

David Higson was considerate, but more than that, he was understanding. He seemed to share my anxieties, which made me feel at one with him. It was not a feeling I was used to.

He kept the conversation focused on me—something that normally didn't happen. It was inherently flattering, and I found myself dropping my guard. Without realizing it, I was moving toward my first relationship with a man in years. And I was too caught up in my own catharsis to even begin to comprehend what was going on with him.

We drove south through the park on 19th Avenue, then turned onto my street. "I'm glad we've been able to get to know each other a little," he said.

I mumbled something about owing it to Gloria, considering I was really tending to her business, and David took exception.

"If she gets the account, it will be because I like your work," he said. "Gloria will just have to be content with doing things our way from now on. As far as I'm concerned, the creative input comes from you." He'd flattered me again—something he did well—while giving every indication of sincerity.

We parked across the street from my apartment. When David acted as though he intended to come in with me, I assumed he wished to review the design package there. I wasn't used to bringing men home with me, and his assumption bothered me for a moment. He was still, after all, a complete stranger.

Then I reminded myself that I had spoken with him at greater length than with any other man in years. I'd bared a part of my soul that even nominal friends hadn't seen.

I lived in a third floor walk-up. David followed me up the stairs. I was quite nervous. Not that my apartment wasn't presentable; I always kept it tidy. But this unmasking process was taking place so fast. I had to stop and ask myself if it was really happening.

I opened the door and David stepped in, looking around with curiosity. My furnishings were eclectic, though pleasant enough. I wasn't accustomed to being judged. However, David put me at ease by heartily expressing his approval. He confided later that from the moment he walked into my apartment he was drawn to it, and to me.

While I excused myself to make coffee, I suddenly remembered how good it felt to connect with a man. I'd spent so many years guarding my heart, I hadn't focused on all I'd been missing.

Once the coffee was ready, we sat down at my small dining room table to drink it. I could see contentment in David's eyes and it made me happy, if only because I was so eager to please. We sipped our coffee in silence for a while before I asked if he was ready to view the now infamous design package.

"I guess that's why I'm here," he said, sounding almost regretful.

I retrieved Gloria's leather portfolio and pulled out the drawings, spreading them across the table. There were several logo designs, letterheads, envelopes, plus the artwork for ComTech's corporate brochures. David studied them with great interest.

"These are wonderful, Allison," he said, holding up two of the logo designs. "Very, very professional."

I was grateful for the compliment. Feedback from clients invariably came through Gloria. She was generous about passing on praise, but it was especially nice to hear it from David.

"You deserve a block of stock for this," he said. "In start-up companies like ours, that's what most people demand in addition to money—the attorneys, the investment bankers, they all want a piece of the action."

"I know ComTech is a high-tech company, but what exactly do you do?"

"We've developed a new chip technology. If successful, it will make us very, very rich. But we're only getting started and our product is still in development."

"How exciting. Computers still seem like a miracle to me. I don't understand them. It must be wonderful, though, to be able to invent something new."

David laughed. "To be honest, Allison, I only have a rudimentary knowledge of computers. I'm the financial guy. My partner, Bob Willis, is the genius. He's the one who invented the concept, and we teamed up to bring it to market."

"You obviously are very successful at what you do."

He leaned back in his chair and looked at me thoughtfully. "I'm on the *verge* of success," he said carefully.

"Because it's a new company?"

"Yes, partly." David grew reflective then. "There's a bit of personal history involved, too," he said.

I wasn't sure if he wanted me to ask him about it, or if he was making an idle comment, so I sipped my coffee and said nothing.

"My family is very wealthy," he explained, staring down at his hands. "I stand to inherit a substantial sum of money. But for several years now, I've wanted to create something of my own, independent of my family."

"That's admirable," I said.

"I haven't succeeded yet."

"You will."

"That's not what I mean," he said, smiling sadly. "Recently, I had to ask my mother and my cousin for help. They control the family business, the Granville Lumber

Company up in Arcata. They agreed to guarantee our bank loan, but my cousin, Dirk, was difficult about it and made certain demands, though on a purely business plane I suppose he was justified. The point is, I'm beholden to them."

David changed the subject then. I assumed his reason for confiding in me was to show that he, too, had suffered. He was trying to find common ground with me. To that extent, he had succeeded. For two very private and lonely people, we'd traveled light-years together in a matter of a few hours.

We returned to our evaluation of the design package. David pronounced himself completely satisfied with my work, saying the drawings could be delivered to the printer. He had only to select the logo design, which he professed would be difficult because he was equally torn between two. He asked my opinion. I did have a favorite and he selected it, saying he trusted my judgment completely.

He looked at me rather nostalgically then, as if he wanted to say more, but was uncertain if he should. I could feel his anxiety.

"What's the matter?" I asked.

"Forgive me for saying this, but you're a pretty woman, Allison. I find you very, very attractive."

I flushed so violently that I'm sure I was crimson.

David noticed, and quickly said he hadn't meant to embarrass me.

"If you only knew," I said with a woeful laugh.

"What do you mean?"

All morning I'd been agonizing, worried that he was reacting to someone who wasn't really me. But now he'd given me a chance to be honest, and I took it. "This isn't really me, David. I don't normally look this way."

He blinked. "What do you mean?"

"The clothes, the makeup. This isn't the person I really am."

He grinned. "What are you trying to say? That you're a fraud?"

I nodded. "Yes, that's exactly right."

He studied me. There was admiration in his eyes. I'd made a terrible admission, and yet he actually seemed pleased. "Are you always so frank?"

"I hate pretense."

"So do I," he said resolutely.

It was hard for me to believe he could be so nice. But I'd gotten myself into another conversational corner, and I was only capable of so much candor at a time. I noticed him fingering his coffee cup. "Can I heat that up for you?" I asked, taking the opportunity to change the subject.

"No, thank you." He contemplated me, then glanced at his watch. "It's too early to go to lunch, but we could go to the park. Do you like to walk in Golden Gate?"

"I do it all the time."

"Me, too." He smiled. "How often do you suppose we've passed each other on the paths?"

"Probably a dozen times."

"No, I don't think so," I said. "I'd have remembered."

"I don't look like this when I walk in the park."

"How do you look?"

"Jeans and an old sweater."

A cocksure expression came over his face. "Why don't you go change?"

It was difficult not to respond to his kindness. David gave me license, brought me out of my shell. How could I not care for him?

I took him up on his offer, figuring he deserved to see me as I really was. I went into my bedroom and changed.

Then I went into the bath, took off my makeup and let down my hair. It fell in waves to well below my shoulders.

I returned to the front room, as afraid as I was determined. I stood at the door for a moment to let him take me in. He rose, looking at me with the same intensity he'd shown when he'd studied my work earlier.

"I've got news for you, Allison," he said, walking over to me. "You're every bit as attractive this way."

I flushed again, knowing it wasn't true. But he made me very happy by saying it. When I lowered my gaze, he lifted my chin and smiled. There was emotion in his eyes. And when he took me by the shoulders, I realized that what I was seeing was desire.

David took a deep breath and pulled me firmly against his body. With another man I might have been shocked, but somehow, with him, I wasn't. By showing his desire, he was telling me he was attracted to the real Allison Stephens. He pressed his lips against my temple, and I put my head on his shoulder.

THE NEXT FEW WEEKS were like a dream. That first day set the pattern. David and I strolled for a long time in the park before it began to sprinkle. Finding ourselves nearer the De Young Museum than my apartment, we went inside. David was no connoisseur of art, but he was willing to learn.

"I admire you for not sticking your nose up at something just because you don't know anything about it," I told him. "So many people are afraid to give art a chance. When you look at a painting or a sculpture, you're seeing the subject through the filter of the artist's own emotions. What you're really seeing is him or her."

He took my hand. "I want to see your art, Allison. I want to see your vision of the world."

His words scared me a little. When you're used to solitude, an intense connection with someone can be a bit overwhelming. I let David hold my hand, though. It brought back that wonderful feeling I used to have with Brandon.

We had a snack at the museum, David suggesting that he take me to dinner instead of out for a big lunch. I didn't hesitate to accept. But David proved to me he had his feet on the ground. He had business calls to make, so at midafternoon he took me home and then went on to his place, promising to return at seven.

I was ready by six-thirty. I put on the violet silk blouse Gloria had given me for Christmas and a gray skirt. And I used some lip gloss and a bit of mascara. I wanted to let David know I cared about my appearance, while still remaining true to myself.

I was pacing in the living room when the telephone rang. It was Gloria, calling from Mexico.

"Oh, my God, Allison," she said, when I told her what had happened. "I don't believe it."

"He loved the design package. That should make you happy."

"Yes, but you're going out with him! That's what's set me on my ear. How wonderful! I'm so happy for you!" The last she said with a squeal of delight.

"Every once in a while I pinch myself," I admitted. "But it's really happening."

"Enjoy yourself," Gloria said, "but it's good strategy to hold back a little. You can't be too careful these days."

Gloria didn't want to offend me by coming right out and saying I was inexperienced. Compared to her, I hadn't been around much, but the warning wasn't necessary.

David was a considerate dinner companion. After he brought me home, we kissed good-night at my door. It wasn't a terribly sexual kiss, but I felt genuine emotion in him. Strangely, I was more aware of his feelings than my own.

I didn't ask him in because I didn't want things to go too fast. I could tell David respected that. And I respected him for caring.

He called the next morning from his office in Santa Clara and asked me out to dinner again. I realized if this were to go on much longer, I would need more to wear. So I went downtown and bought several outfits, splurging on clothes for the first time ever.

I felt like a snake that had shed its old skin. But even as I felt myself changing, I was aware that I valued my relationship with David more than I valued David himself. That might seem strange, but in a way it was a compliment to him. I identified with David Higson, and I believed in the end that would prove to be even more important than love.

We were intimate for the first time that weekend. David stayed over after we'd gone to a Moroccan restaurant. I opened a bottle of dessert sherry I'd had on the shelf forever and we both got a bit tipsy.

He kissed me more energetically than before, then he led me into my bedroom. We undressed in silence. I was nervous, so I got under the covers, shivering from the cold sheets. David's body was warm and, when he touched me, drawing his hand up the inside of my thigh, I realized how much of a void there'd been in my life.

David was unselfish enough to arouse me. He took his time and made me want him. And though he was large and physically dominating, at the moment of his greatest excitement, I was aware of the care he took, his unwillingness to hurt me in any way.

Afterward he held me close and kissed my face, whispering how wonderful I was. I'd heard that before, from other men, but David seemed to mean it. And I realized then that David Higson was already falling in love with me.

3

SEX WAS AN IMPORTANT part of our relationship, though it was never pivotal for either of us. David loved me deeply and soon told me so. I held back emotionally, partly out of a need to be cautious, but also because my feelings were complicated.

When Gloria got back from Mexico, she and I had a long talk. "You're approaching this maturely," she said after I'd brought her up to date on what had been happening. "Lord knows, I wish I could do the same. I still expect whistles and bells to go off when I get in bed with a man. You're wise to use your head."

Gloria was trying to be supportive, to make the best of what she considered merely a comfortable relationship. But she didn't understand that "comfortable" was important to me. A man who gave without demanding too much in return might be the best kind, I reasoned. Besides, I had a great deal of respect for David.

So I did nothing to discourage him. We saw each other almost daily. A few times he had business obligations that kept him in Santa Clara until late. And there were some evenings when he showed up bone tired. I would make dinner and we would talk or watch television before going to bed.

One night, I sketched him while he was reading the *Wall Street Journal*. I fixed him the Scotch and soda he liked after a hard day, then sat on the ottoman to draw.

When I'd finished, I showed David the picture. He said it was good, but he had a funny look on his face as he stared at it. I asked him what was wrong.

"It's strange," he said, "but I can see my father in this picture. I never thought of myself as looking like him, but I guess I must."

"When will I meet your family?" I asked.

David brushed my cheek with his fingers. "Probably not for a while. My family's not one of the happier aspects of my life," he said.

I accepted the words at face value, for I assumed I knew David. And in ways, of course, I did. But there was a side to him I didn't know—a side he kept hidden. And his family was the key to discovering that other self.

So I didn't press him, hoping that everything would work out eventually. To my utter surprise, I found it incredibly easy to adjust to our relationship. I never felt closed in. David gave me space. That, and the fact that I felt he understood me, made all the difference.

In early November David proposed. We had just made love and were lying side by side, holding hands. I had been staring at the raindrops on the windowpane, made silvery from the lamppost outside my building, when he said, "Allison, I want to ask you something."

I turned toward him. Even in the shadows of my darkened room I could see how sober his expression was. I knew he was about to say something momentous.

"People shouldn't marry unless they're at a settled stage in their lives," he began, "and I'm really struggling with ComTech right now. But I don't want to wait. I want you to be my wife." He took a deep breath. "Will you marry me?"

I didn't know what to say, so I kissed him. After a minute he said, "You don't have to give me an answer now. I know this is sudden."

I thought it over during the weekend, without having serious doubts about what I would do. I was nearly thirty-seven and well beyond illusion. The comfort, companionship and understanding he brought me were not easily denied. So that Sunday, I told David I would marry him.

"I'm so happy for you," Gloria said, when I told her the news. "It's all so fabulous. Why, only a few weeks ago I was lamenting leaving you behind when I went off to Mexico for my romantic adventure."

Gloria hadn't said much about her trip, but I knew there'd been a disappointment of some kind. Then, soon after her return, she began talking about a lawyer named Don Something-or-other, whom she'd briefly dated the summer before. Gloria used our engagement as an excuse to set up a dinner date for the four of us, in part so that she could see David and me together.

Don turned out to be slender and angular, a tennis devotee when he wasn't playing lawyer. He was nice enough, if a little overbearing. He had the habit of constantly brushing a hank of his thin blond hair off his forehead. He had a favorite Mexican restaurant out on Geary, which is where David and I met them.

We were a little late because David had gotten caught in traffic coming up the Peninsula. Gloria looked at David with a curious anxiety, and for the first time ever I thought I saw a spark of jealousy in my friend's eyes. She had wanted to find someone like David for the longest time, only to see me stumble into what she so desperately coveted.

Don soon exceeded his limit on margaritas and, to Gloria's obvious annoyance, monopolized the conversation.

David politely endured him. After we'd finished our meal, Gloria and I escaped to the ladies' room.

"David is really very nice," she told me. "I'm so happy for you, Allison. And he seems really fond of you. I can tell he's in love."

"He says he loves me."

She took my hands in hers. "Do you love him?"

I nodded, trying to smile through my embarrassment.

"This falling-in-love business can be overrated," Gloria said, "but there has to be something between people if they're going to make a go of marriage."

"David has made me happy," I said with a sigh. "He's good to me and I enjoy his company. And we have a lot in common."

"No one is more deserving," she told me, a tiny quaver in her voice. "Have you set a date?"

"David wants to marry before the holidays."

"My, he doesn't let the grass grow under his feet, does he?"

"It's our age," I said. "He's forty-four and I'm almost thirty-seven. David says if we're going to do it, we shouldn't fritter away our time."

Gloria looked skeptical. "Neither of you are kids, but is that a reason to rush? Unless you're desperate to have children, why not take your time? Enjoy yourself for a while and really get to know each other."

"You think I'm making a mistake, don't you?" I said.

"It's not that," she replied. "It's just that I've had several relationships that seemed so perfect at first. Time was telling in each case."

"I'm not kidding myself, Gloria," I told her. "I don't even think in terms of perfect. I only know David makes me feel good. I could meet a thousand men before I found that again."

Gloria didn't say anything more. She just gave me a hug.

During the following weeks, I thought about our future almost constantly. All I had to do was compare the way things were with the way they'd been. That seemed to me the most relevant consideration.

I was so wrapped up in myself that the telltale signs of David's problems sailed right over my head. He may have made a halfhearted effort to alert me to what was happening at ComTech, but he never laid out the situation clearly.

Frankly, I don't know if it would have mattered. I had never thought of him in terms of financial security, and his degree of success wasn't important to me. What I didn't comprehend was how important it was to him.

David worked terribly hard. There were even telephone calls in the evening that he preferred to take in the privacy of my bedroom. "Trying to make a success of a start-up company can be hell," he said one night after a half-hour phone call. "I'm sorry that took so long, Allison."

We were in the kitchen, and I was fixing him a Scotch. I set the glass on the counter, then put my arms around him. "I don't like to see you so stressed out."

"Money and family never mix," he said, his tone uncharacteristically bitter.

Family again. There was a hardness in his eyes. I'd never seen David like that before.

"Who were you talking to?" I asked.

"It's not important."

"But you seem upset."

"It's not your problem," he said sharply.

I must have blinked. I know I was shocked. David had never spoken to me that way before. "All right," I said, "if you don't want to share your troubles, I won't insist."

He put his hand on my shoulder. "I'm sorry, honey. I don't talk about my family because I don't want them to interfere in our relationship."

"But once we're married, they'll be my family, too," I protested.

"My cousin is in a category by himself. But let's not discuss it anymore," he said, abruptly ending the conversation.

Just before Thanksgiving we made our engagement official by buying a ring. That evening we were sitting on the sofa. David was reading his paper and I was staring at my diamond.

"It seems as if somebody should enjoy this besides us," I said. "It's too bad we aren't going to be with your family for Thanksgiving."

"Mother is the only one who counts," David replied. "This isn't a good time."

"Then when will I get to meet her?"

"Probably not until after the wedding."

David wanted to leave our plans vague, a point of frustration for me. I assumed that was because he hadn't decided what to do about his family, but it did come as a shock that he didn't even want them involved. "Don't you want your mother to attend?"

"It would be difficult, considering her condition. Besides, Mother doesn't like to leave home, and I certainly don't want to get married up there."

David's mother was an invalid, wheelchair-bound and living with her housekeeper in the big old Victorian house on the coast north of Arcata. He never revealed more than that, so I had no idea what she was like. I made him put his paper down.

"David, tell me about your mother."

He did not look pleased. For a moment he stared off, clearly deliberating over what to divulge and what to keep hidden. "She's willful," he said. "Her home and her heritage are everything to her. My mother is one of the more prideful people alive."

"You must be important to her, as well," I replied.

"We have an understanding," he said evasively.

I could tell he didn't want to say more. He seemed determined to keep certain things buried in his heart. "Will you tell me about your cousin, then?" I asked, hoping to exploit the small opening David had given me.

"Dirk is the last person on earth I care to discuss," he responded coldly.

"I don't mean to upset you," I told him, "but surely you understand my curiosity."

He folded his paper and put it down. His expression was one of resignation, but also pique. "One of the things that appealed to me about you, Allison, is that you're not demanding. I've felt from the beginning that we understood each other."

"We do," I protested, anguish rising in me.

"I haven't asked you a lot of questions," he said, "because I knew that would justify your questions to me. But I suppose I can understand how my preference for privacy might be misunderstood."

"It is not my intent to pry," I insisted.

"I know. You want to know what sort of family you're marrying into."

"That's not unreasonable."

"Okay. I'll tell you about them, but I don't want to be pressured for more information in the future."

"I understand."

He told me then how his grandfather had purchased a lumber mill during the Great Depression, subsequently making a fortune. When the old man died, David's mother, Edwina, and her younger sister, Sarah, inherited everything. And David's father, Morris Higson, ran the business.

Sarah died at an early age, leaving her interest in the mill to her young son, Dirk Granville. Edwina and Morris dreamed that David would eventually take over the company, and for a time David did work for his father, but it turned out to be a horrible experience. Disillusioned, he went off to make his own fortune. He didn't go into detail, but I gathered that Morris Higson had been a tyrant.

"The real crisis came when my father died," David explained. "Dirk was already in control of his half of the stock. Then my mother made a deal with him, virtually putting the company in his hands. She later wrote me, saying that my time would come when she died. Still, I felt betrayed."

I was beginning to understand David's bitterness. But I sensed it wasn't his mother he blamed so much as his cousin. "There's no love lost between you and Dirk, is there?" I said.

David hooted. "The bastard has never recognized my competence. He thought I was weak just because I didn't stand up to my father the way he did. But he never understood that being a nephew isn't the same as being a son."

The depth of his bitterness astounded me. I could see now why his family was best kept at a distance. "I'm sure your mother anguishes over this," I said, trying to be reassuring.

"My mother is a wonderful woman, very strong," he said. "But she has never understood how important it is for me to be my own person, to control my own destiny."

I could see now why the loan he'd talked about had become such a troublesome matter. We didn't discuss his family again. It was understood that our wedding would not involve them, but that sometime afterward he would take me to Arcata to meet his mother.

"Have you told her about me?" I asked one Sunday. "Does she even know we're engaged?"

"No," David replied. "I haven't figured out when and how I will tell her."

I resolved to ask no more questions. Every relationship had its problems. David's family could be a major one for us only if we let it. But I wasn't marrying his family, I was marrying him. My husband-to-be was making his own life and I was determined to stand behind him—if necessary, against his own family.

DAVID AND I WERE TO BE married at the beginning of December. We decided on a small wedding and were left only with the task of figuring out where to have it.

Gloria's widowed mother had a beautiful home in Seacliff that overlooked the Golden Gate Bridge and the Pacific. She wintered in Hawaii, and told Gloria she would be happy to make her place available for the ceremony, insisting it would be no imposition since it was to be a such small affair. I think she considered it a tune-up for Gloria's moment in the sun. Regardless, I was grateful for her generosity.

Despite her misgivings, Gloria cheerfully assumed the role of mother of the bride. Since she had a strong sense of organization, I was relieved to have her help. We consulted David, but for the most part he left everything up to us.

The invitation list was short. In addition to Gloria, I invited two friends from U.S.F., and two others I'd met

after college. One of the four was married and another
brought a date. Gloria asked her lawyer friend, Don, to
escort her. That made eight guests of the bride.

David's friends were almost entirely business acquain-
tances. Though he didn't feel sufficient personal rapport
to invite them to his wedding, I wanted him to have someone there and urged him to invite Robert Willis, his business partner, as a minimum. He reluctantly agreed.

As our wedding day grew near, I felt badly about the
absence of his family, though I never brought the matter
up. I feared his mother might someday hold me responsible, but I knew better than to interfere.

The last week before the big day David was so distracted that I grew concerned. Deep down I feared he was
having second thoughts. But he assured me his concerns
were purely business in nature. Things had gotten very
difficult at ComTech, he said.

We planned to go to Cabo San Lucas for our wedding
trip—not ostentatious, but it would cost us a few dollars.
I asked if we shouldn't consider putting off the trip, but
David insisted we couldn't marry without a honeymoon.

"Would you like to delay the wedding, then?" I asked.
"At least until things settle down at the office?"

"No, Allison," he said, taking me into his arms. "I don't
know of anything I've ever wanted more than marrying
you. And I won't have it put off." He kissed me with more
passion than was usual then, and I believed him—perhaps because I wanted to with all my heart.

When I awoke the morning of our wedding, a Saturday, it was raining. Gloria and I had stayed at her mother's house as a nod toward tradition. Climbing out of bed,
I looked out at the gray waters of the bay and across the
Golden Gate Bridge at the Marin headlands, truncated by
the dark, leaden clouds. It was not the sort of weather I'd

hoped for, but in a matter of hours we would be off to sunny Mexico, so it didn't really matter.

At breakfast Gloria bemoaned the weather, but I told her I didn't believe in omens. I was born, my father had told me in one of our rare conversations, on a beautiful sunny day in May. It did not turn out to be an auspicious one for either my mother or me.

By late morning, the skies had cleared somewhat. That pleased Gloria, so for that reason I was glad. The ceremony was scheduled for five, with a champagne reception and catered buffet afterward. David and I would spend our wedding night at home, then fly out early the next morning.

I had selected a champagne satin cocktail dress with long sleeves and a modest scoop neck as my bridal gown. When I gazed at myself in the mirror, I realized I truly looked like a bride.

During the final minutes before the ceremony, I stood at the big picture window in the master bedroom and watched the clouds close in again. Raindrops started falling, smearing the pane. In that quiet moment, I thought of the mother I'd never known. I don't recall ever crying for her before, but I did then.

When Gloria came for me, I wiped my eyes, found my smile and went downstairs to where our guests, the judge and my husband-to-be were gathered. Standing next to David, I slipped my arm in his. At precisely that moment, it began raining as heavily as I have ever seen. Thunder— something rarely heard in San Francisco—rolled in from the Pacific.

Undeterred, the judge commenced his introductory remarks. I squeezed David's fingers, praying for happiness. It was strange, but something told me that my prayers might not be answered.

4

IN THE SUNSHINE OF Cabo San Lucas I began to relax. At first I thought David, too, had begun to forget the problems we'd left behind. He was attentive and affectionate, but there were moments when he was off somewhere, distracted. We'd be sitting across from each other at dinner, or walking on the beach, when a glazed, faraway look would come into his eyes.

I ignored it for a while. Then, on about the third day, I asked him about it. We were in beach chairs under a huge white umbrella, watching the rollers coming in. "Are you worried about business, David?"

"I'm sorry if I seem preoccupied," he said.

I wouldn't let him off the hook. "It must be a lot worse than you're letting on." For the first time, I assumed a wifely prerogative. "I wish you wouldn't try to spare me. We must deal with whatever it is together."

He admitted that he was in jeopardy of losing everything. Robert Willis's technological innovation had developed a hitch, meaning a time delay. Worse, a competitor had come up with a similar innovation, and they were much further along, meaning that ComTech could be frozen out of the marketplace.

The situation was grave. I struggled to recall what David had said about his loan—especially his family's involvement. Something told me that was worrying him even more than the loss of ComTech.

"We should have put off the wedding," I said flatly.

David shook his head. "No, you're the only good thing that's happened to me lately. If I didn't have you, I'd be lost."

I saw desperation in his eyes. David's business problems hadn't exactly been a secret, but exchanging long looks now, I suddenly saw something new. My husband had begun relying on me for emotional support. He was telling me that he needed me. Badly.

WE RETURNED TO San Francisco to discover that tragedy had struck during our absence. Robert Willis had been killed in an automobile accident, destroying any hope of ComTech's recovery. It was a mortal blow.

When David gave me the news, I was afraid for him. I knew now how essential his business was to his self-image and I worried that the setback might even destroy his confidence.

But he was more stoic than I would have guessed. Maybe he'd been worried for so long that the final blow came as a relief.

He sat in my old green chair, staring into space, his mind a million miles away. I'd brought him a Scotch and silently watched as he sipped it. I couldn't help wondering if this strange serenity was a danger signal.

I decided it was my duty to be strong, and resolved not to let my concern show. I was still working for Gloria, though at a slower pace than before.

But much to my surprise, ComTech's problems did not mark the end of David's labors. He said he still had obligations, so he spent long hours in Santa Clara, frequently not returning until late at night.

It seemed as if our marriage was put on hold while David worked through his difficulties. I became his emotional prop. There was little direct conversation between us on the subject, but I sensed how important it was to him to know he could come home and find me there, a smile on my face, not demanding or criticizing or accusing.

David never discussed the loan guarantee his family had made. Would he be personally obligated to pay back the money? If so, I speculated that was a worry to him. I talked around the subject, hoping he would tell me what was going on, but he never did. And I was hurt when he didn't take me into his confidence.

The trip to Arcata was dropped. This bothered me, especially considering the loan guarantee. It seemed to me that dealing with his family had become even more urgent. I worried constantly about slighting them. Finally, at the beginning of Christmas week, I was so frustrated I decided to ask David about it.

He'd come home late, around eleven, and I was already in bed, though I was reading. He was standing at the closet, stooped with fatigue, as he undressed.

"David," I said, "have you given any thought to going up to Arcata?"

"Some," he said, noncommittally.

"With Christmas a few days away, I thought maybe it would be a good time to visit your mother. After all, she has a daughter-in-law she hasn't met. And I would like to meet her."

"I think that should wait until the dust settles at ComTech," he said.

"She and your cousin must be upset about that, too," I said. "Doesn't Robert's death affect the loan they guaranteed?"

David looked at me darkly and said, "Let me worry about that, Allison. It's none of your affair."

Tears welled, but I found the courage to snap back, "I'm your wife, aren't I? Don't you think your family matters to me? Just because you haven't had the decency to introduce me to them doesn't mean I don't care!"

I began crying. I had tried so hard not to let David's problems affect me, but suddenly I felt the weight of everything closing in on me—the difficult first days of our marriage, David's financial worries, his family obligations. Once the emotion came out, I started weeping uncontrollably.

David sat down beside me, taking me into his arms. "Don't cry, Allison," he said. "Please don't cry. Everything will be all right."

"How can you say that?" I said between sobs. "Do you know something I don't?"

He sighed and stroked my head. I was clutching the front of his shirt, my heart aching. I felt everything was hopeless, even though he seemed to understand my misery.

"I'm sorry," I sniffed. "You've got more than enough problems already." I reached for a tissue on the nightstand. I blew my nose and wiped my eyes. When I'd finished, I found David looking at me gravely.

"Don't worry about my family," he said, his tone sober. "They're taken care of. Dirk saw to that."

"What do you mean?"

"One of the conditions of the loan guarantee was that ComTech take out a key-man policy on Bob's life. Dirk was well aware that Bob's creative genius was the company's principal asset."

"You mean there was insurance money?"

"Yes. If Granville Lumber winds up having to make good on the bank loan—which will probably be the case—Dirk and my mother will come out whole."

"That's good, isn't it?"

"Certainly. The last thing I want is to see our family business hurt. I have a stake in that, too, albeit a future stake."

"That must make you feel better," I said hopefully.

David nodded, though there was no joy on his face, or even relief. He still seemed troubled.

I put my hand on his arm. "I know the loss of ComTech is a blow," I told him. "But you'll find another company, something else to do."

He smiled at my naiveté. I had no profound understanding of business and we both knew it. But it was my duty as a wife to be supportive, and I think he appreciated that.

"There's not a lot I can do to help," I said, "but I believe in you, David. I want you to know that."

He pulled me against him then, holding my head to his chest. "Don't think about them, Allison," he muttered. "It's better if you don't." He wasn't being responsive, and I wasn't sure what he meant, unless he was talking about his family again. "You're my rock," he went on, rambling. "The only time I'm happy is when I'm with you. You've got nothing to do with any of them. Let me worry about it. I've got a plan. It will be all right."

David seemed almost in a daze. The detached lucidity I'd associated with him from the start was gone. I realized then that my husband was barely holding himself together. He'd become a different person.

THE LAST DAYS BEFORE Christmas were tense. David was coping, but barely, and I was afraid for him.

We spent Christmas Day alone, though midmorning he went into the bedroom to call his mother. He related none of the conversation except to say that she was looking forward to meeting me. I had no way of knowing if that was true, but I was not about to make an issue of it. This one day, I decided, we would find what joy we could. We were, after all, newlyweds.

Gloria dropped by in the middle of the afternoon and we exchanged gifts. I'd made some eggnog and David pulled himself together enough to play the good host. He served it cordially, seeming for a while like his old self. It made me happy, and I almost forgot about our problems. It was the best I'd felt about us since our return from Mexico.

David went to the office late the next morning, promising it would be a short day. I puttered around the apartment. Things tended to slow down in the commercial-design business over the holidays, so I got out my oils and set up my easel for the first time in months.

My studio was crowded now because the extra bedroom was doing double duty as David's office. I didn't mind sharing, and it was certainly a small price to pay to have him around a little more.

I worked happily, priming canvas and experimenting with an abstract piece. In the middle of the afternoon, the downstairs buzzer sounded. I assumed it was Gloria, but the caller turned out to be an insurance investigator by the name of Paul Davis. He wanted to ask a few routine questions about Robert Willis. I buzzed him in, though I knew it was doubtful I would be of much help.

Davis, a middle-aged man with thinning hair and longish sideburns, handed me his card. I looked at it perfunctorily, noticing that he was wearing a rather worn-looking brown suit. I indicated a chair and he sat down, seeming bored even before he began.

"Did you know Robert Willis very well, Mrs. Higson?" he asked without preamble.

"I only met him once, to be honest. At my wedding."

"You and Mr. Higson are recently married, then?"

"Yes, about three weeks ago."

"Oh, newlyweds. Congratulations."

"Thank you."

"Then, that was the only time you saw Willis?"

"That's right."

On several occasions I'd thought about my husband's partner, though naturally I'd had other things on my mind the day of the wedding. Still, he'd been David's only friend in attendance, so during the reception I'd made an effort to reach out to him.

Robert Willis had struck me as strange. He'd been around fifty, and had appeared rather scholarly. He had worn thick glasses and I remembered him as being reluctant to make eye contact. He had few social skills and had been very quiet, speaking up only once when he'd offered his congratulations. He'd been the first to leave, and I remembered feeling sorry for him.

"You wouldn't have any feeling for whether the guy might have been suicidal, would you, Mrs. Higson?" the investigator asked.

The question took me by surprise. "No, I don't. We only spoke for a few minutes."

"I see."

"Is there some reason to think it was suicide?" I asked. "I was under the impression he was in an automobile accident."

"Willis went off the cliff down at Devil's Slide, by Pacifica, late at night. Nobody saw it, so we gotta ask questions, you know. When a guy's worth four million dollars dead, an insurance company likes to be sure what happened."

"*Four* million?"

"That's right."

"I had no idea."

"This guy Willis must have been pretty hot stuff."

"My husband said he was a genius."

"He must have been, all right." Davis had a pen and a small notebook in his hand, but he hadn't yet written anything. "Tell me, Mrs. Higson, did your husband ever indicate that Willis was suicidal? Ever hear any talk along those lines?"

"No, nothing like that at all."

"No mention of things going badly at ComTech?"

"I was aware generally that they were having difficulties, but nothing was ever said about Robert being depressed."

"Okay. Anything else that might make you think this trip off the cliff wasn't an accident?" he asked.

"No, there isn't. But I'm not sure why you're asking me these questions. You should really talk to David and the other people in the company."

"Oh, we are, Mrs. Higson. Four million makes us do a lot of asking." He wrote indifferently in his notebook. "What were the problems at ComTech, Mrs. Higson? What can you tell me?"

"You're asking the wrong person, Mr. Davis. My husband can give you the answers to your questions."

"What has Mr. Higson told you?"

I found his pressing annoying and decided to end the interview. "David rarely discusses business with me. I know almost nothing about Robert Willis or the insurance policy."

"Did you ever discuss the policy with Dirk Granville or Edwina Higson?"

"I've never met Mr. Granville, let alone discussed insurance with him. My mother-in-law is an invalid and I haven't as yet had the opportunity of meeting her. David and I plan to go to Arcata soon. So at this point, I'm afraid I can't help you."

The insurance investigator flipped his notebook shut. "Well, I believe I've imposed on you enough, Mrs. Higson. Thank you for your time."

He got up, and I followed him to the door.

"Is this normal procedure?" I asked. "This questioning?"

He gave me a half smile and said, "For this kind of money, it is."

That evening, when I told David about the visit, he was visibly annoyed, though he soon regained his calm. "The policy stands to cost them a lot," he said. "They're scratching around to see if there's a way out."

"Is suicide exempt from the policy?" I asked.

"A portion of the policy carries double indemnity in the event of an accidental death. They may be trying to beat that. I've been pressing for payment, so I suspect this is a last-ditch effort. I'm sorry you had to deal with it, Allison."

"More than anything, I was embarrassed that I knew so little."

"There's nothing to know," he said before falling silent. After a minute he said, "Let's not think about that. Hopefully it will be all over soon and we can concentrate on us. You've been deprived."

"Nonsense," I replied. "We have a lifetime to look forward to. I know how critical these days are for you."

David kissed my hair. But then one of those distant looks came over his face, and he didn't say anything for a while. I hoped whatever was troubling him would be over soon, but for some reason I wasn't confident that it would. I sensed that something was wrong and that the tragedy of Robert Willis was only the beginning.

OVER THE NEXT FEW WEEKS, David's hours became much more reasonable. There were days when he didn't bother driving down to Santa Clara at all. But whenever he stayed home he was edgy, occasionally going for solitary walks in the park while I worked at my drafting table. Gloria had brought me two big projects that kept me busy, though I tried to make myself available if David wished to talk. Most of the time he maintained a brooding silence, which worried me.

On a couple of occasions he made phone calls and then would rush off somewhere, saying he had business to tend to. He would return a few hours later, usually in a black mood. There were other times when I was alone and the phone would ring. When I answered it, nobody would be there. I mentioned this to David and he brushed it aside, saying it was probably a wrong number.

I tried to be patient and cheerful. Whenever I directed our conversations to his business problems, he would quickly shut me off. After avoiding the subject for a couple of weeks, at dinner one evening I again raised the question of our trip to Arcata.

"Not yet," he said abruptly. "That will have to wait."

It was only a few days later that David announced that he had business to tend to in Arcata, but that he would be making the trip alone. It wasn't the best time to deal with family matters, he said. I was hurt by his announcement, and told him so.

"I know how you feel, Allison, but I'm under a lot of pressure and I've got to do this alone. But I'll talk to my mother about a visit by the two of us. We'll do it soon. I promise."

I hated to be difficult, so I let it pass. Over a week had gone by since we'd made love. Whatever was going on was tearing at the heart of our marriage.

The night before he left, David held me in his arms, realizing how badly my heart was aching. He proceeded to tell me how sorry he was that things had been so difficult. Then he told me that he loved me, and that what troubled him most was that he hadn't been a success for me, that he'd brought me nothing but worry.

"David," I said, my eyes welling with tears, "I don't care about money or success. I just want us to be happy. As long as we have our health and each other, what else matters?"

He kissed my forehead. "I love you for your goodness, Allison. That was one of the things that drew me to you. You are a wonderful wife."

I can't say that I didn't believe David, because I did. But I knew then—that last night we were together—that something in him had altered. He was a different man.

For a while we lay in silence, aware of each other but mute. Then David rolled onto his side, facing me. He touched my cheek with his finger. "I know the last month has been crazy. You've been hurt. But I promise you one day it will be different."

He put his hand under my gown and began stroking my thigh. I wasn't feeling sexy, but I couldn't deny him.

David continued caressing me, but I didn't feel anything. Then I did something I hadn't done before. I began to think about Brandon, fantasizing about him. My body began responding immediately and I felt guilty about that. It was as though I was being unfaithful to the man I'd scarcely been married to a month.

David was aware of my growing excitement. I tried to put Brandon out of my mind, but I couldn't. When David finally moved on top of me, spreading my legs, I began to cry silently, hating myself, hating the terrible misfortune that had beset us.

David, too, seemed to be struggling. There was a sadness in him, a poignant regret. I could tell that he was anguished. He hated what had happened as much as I did. Yet I also knew he loved me.

When he finally came, I squeezed him to my breast as tears ran down the sides of my face and into my hair. He murmured that he loved me and kissed my shoulder.

In the morning we had breakfast together. David acted ill at ease, and tried to make small talk, filling the time as people do before goodbyes. At the door he gave me a hard, emotional kiss and said again that he loved me. There may even have been tears in his eyes, though I can't say for sure. It was almost as if he knew he wouldn't be coming back.

I slept terribly that night. Around noon the next day two police officers, a man and a woman, came to my door to tell me that my husband had drowned in a boating accident in Humboldt Bay. That kiss he'd given me at the door of my apartment was to be our last.

5

THE POLICE OFFICERS stayed for a while. I asked them to call Gloria and she arrived half an hour later. I was still in shock when she got there, focusing on what had happened just long enough to cry for a bit, but then my mind lapsed into a state of denial. I paced, certain there'd been a mistake, that my new life couldn't be ending so soon.

After the officers left, Gloria phoned the Humboldt County sheriff's department for the latest information while I sat in my old green chair, nearly catatonic. We were told that David's battered kayak had been found just inside the mouth of the bay. He'd been seen going out into the surf, but he'd never returned. His car was found parked along the South Jetty Road, his street clothes in the trunk, his wallet under the seat. Gloria asked what he'd been doing, going out in a kayak in January. They told her he'd been fishing. That really brought home the unreality of it all. I hadn't even known my husband was a fisherman.

Gloria spent that night with me. The next morning she called the sheriff for an update. David's body still hadn't washed ashore, and the fear was that it had been swept out to sea. It could be days or weeks before it turned up. It might never be recovered.

It was then that I thought of David's family. I decided it was my place to contact them, so I went through his desk, looking for his mother's number. When I found it, I telephoned.

The housekeeper told me that Mrs. Higson was under sedation. She suggested that I might wish to talk to Dirk Granville. She gave me a number. I was reluctant to make contact with David's old enemy, but knew I had no choice. I was relieved when I got an answering machine. After hesitating, I left my name and number.

Gloria insisted on staying with me another night, though I told her it wasn't necessary. My friend, who'd been surrogate mother of the bride, had now become surrogate mother of the grieving widow.

An unexpected death does not easily become a reality. I could not think of David as dead. And yet, when I told myself he was gone, the pain and heartache would nearly overwhelm me. It struck me as so much crueller that fate should give him to me for a few months, then snatch him away. How much kinder it would have been to have left me in my solitude.

That afternoon, while Gloria did some work over the telephone with Karen, I lay down for a nap. To my surprise I fell into a deep sleep. It was dark when I awoke to the ringing of the phone. Gloria must have taken the call on the extension in the kitchen because the ringing stopped.

I lay still for several moments. David's death seeped back into my brain like a caustic acid. Then Gloria opened the door a crack and peered into the darkness.

"Are you awake, Allison?" she whispered.

"Yes."

"There's a call for you. It's Mr. Granville."

I sat bolt upright as fear stabbed my heart. In spite of my earlier call, I didn't really want to speak to Dirk. Ever since David had recounted his family history, I'd shared his bitterness toward his cousin. Dirk had triumphed at

David's expense and I resented him for that, without even knowing him.

I turned on the bedside lamp and swung my legs off the bed, collecting my thoughts before picking up the receiver. Gloria withdrew, closing the door. I pressed the phone to my ear and nervously listened for a moment before saying, "Hello?"

"Allison, this is Dirk Granville." He said my name with such assurance that I was put off, annoyed even.

"Yes, Mr. Granville."

"I'm sorry about what's happened. It's a terrible thing. I know you're suffering."

I didn't believe him. I suspected he was secretly pleased. After all, with David gone, he had no competition. Everything was his—including, perhaps, millions in insurance money. "I'm still in a daze," I said. "You'll have to forgive me."

He sighed. "I know it's difficult to make decisions at a time like this, but some things will have to be decided soon. I'll do whatever I can from this end to make things easier for you."

Dirk Granville had a resonant, sensual voice and that surprised me. I'd expected something harsher, more in keeping with the hard mental image I had of him. "I appreciate your consideration," I said carefully.

"I'm afraid my aunt is still in shock. So if you need help in making arrangements, I'm probably the best one to deal with."

How little that prospect appealed to me! I wanted to tell David's cousin that it would be all right with me if we never even met. I knew it was unfair to think that, but I had already decided Dirk Granville was partly to blame for what had happened. He might not have been directly responsible, but he'd clearly had a hand in David's misery over the years, and I was sure in my heart that my husband had died because of his unhappiness. Even if it had been an accident, his state of mind had to have been a factor.

"Is there something in particular you wish to suggest?" I asked. "Presumably you're talking about a funeral. Does Mrs. Higson have a preference as to what should be done?"

"That's a little premature," he said. "The body hasn't been recovered yet. But I'm sure Aunt Edwina will want to know what you plan once the time comes."

There was no hostility at all in Dirk Granville's voice. I can't even say it sounded cold or uncaring. Yet I sensed that there were ulterior motives beneath the politeness; maybe he was even an adversary. It did briefly occur to me I was reading too much into the situation, that the intensity of my emotions had me confused, but I was wary just the same.

"Please tell Mrs. Higson that I will be sensitive to her wishes," I said, my voice trembling ever so slightly. "I know David was her son and that she must have suggestions as to how things are handled."

"She'll be very grateful for that, I know," he replied. "Once she's recovered from the immediate shock, I'm sure she'll want to see you. It may be premature to discuss it now, but I thought I should mention it."

My eyes began to fill with tears. How tragically sad that plans were finally being made for me to meet David's mother—now that he was dead and we had nothing to share but the loss. "Please tell her I'd be happy to come and see her," I said.

"Why don't I contact you in a few days to make arrangements?" he said. "Everybody needs a little time alone right now, I think. It's good we've talked, though. I know my aunt will have questions about you and I want to be able to answer them."

It occurred to me that Dirk Granville might have questions about me himself. As David's widow I would have to be dealt with about so many things. I considered telling the man that he had no reason to be concerned about me, that I had no desire for anything that was David's. But I wasn't up to a lengthy conversation.

"Is there anything at all I can do for you, Allison?" he asked.

"No. Thank you. There's nothing."

"Well, if something comes up, let me know."

"Yes, I will."

I hung up, Dirk Granville's low, sensuous tones still ringing in my ears. I was curious about him. I speculated whether he was insincere, devious and conniving; whether he cared about me as he'd said; whether he was concerned about anything apart from protecting his own interests. I instantly decided that he couldn't be trusted and that I didn't like him.

After running a comb through my hair, I went to the kitchen. Gloria was standing at the stove, looking completely out of her element. But she was there for me, and I was deeply grateful.

"How are you doing?" she asked, putting down a wooden spoon.

"Terrible."

She came over and took my hands, then led me to the small table where David and I'd had breakfast that last morning. "So, what did Mr. Granville want?" she asked as we both sat down.

I related the gist of the conversation.

"It's the polite thing to do," she said.

"Maybe, but I don't like the man."

"Why?"

"He made life very difficult for David, so he's at least partly responsible for what happened."

Her eyes widened. "You mean his drowning?"

"I mean his misery. David was terribly unhappy this last month. He was like a man possessed. And what's so sad is, I never felt I could do anything to help him."

I hadn't told Gloria about any of the problems at ComTech, so I gave her a brief account of what I knew, which wasn't a lot. My eyes bubbled with tears when the realization again struck that David was gone, that he had passed away without having achieved the success that he'd so badly wanted.

Gloria patted my hands, but I was thinking about David's final words to me, his expression of love. I began crying, feeling my life had been shattered, right along with his.

I pulled myself together and helped Gloria finish dinner. While we were eating, a reporter from one of the San Francisco papers called. She noted that the two principals of ComTech had died in tragic accidents within a very short time and wanted to know if I thought there might be some connection. The question caught me off guard and I asked what she was getting at.

"ComTech was in serious trouble, Mrs. Higson. There are stories that big insurance payments have resulted from the deaths."

"There was a policy on Robert Willis," I told her, "but all that did was secure a company loan. No one gained by it."

"Was there a policy on your husband's life, too?"

"To be honest, I don't know. David certainly never mentioned one to me."

"Really?"

The reporter was goading me and being pushy. Maybe that was her job, but I couldn't help being offended by her insensitivity. "I really don't wish to discuss this with you," I said.

"I'm doing a story on ComTech," she replied, "and I thought you might like the opportunity to clear up any questions that might be out there."

"I'm not sure what you're suggesting."

"I'm not suggesting anything, Mrs. Higson. I just want to find out what might have been going on behind the scenes."

I began shaking with emotion. "Talk to Dirk Granville, my husband's cousin, if you have questions about that," I said with a trembling voice. "I don't have any information that could be of help to you." Then I hung up the phone.

Gloria had heard the conversation, and she was outraged on my behalf. "Those people can be so thoughtless."

I sat there, wiping my eyes. "It does bring home a point, Gloria. I know virtually nothing about David's business. I couldn't even tell that reporter whether he was insured or not. I felt like such a fool."

"It was a new marriage and you'd both led very independent lives beforehand. Those things take time."

I took a minute to think about our financial situation. A couple of weeks before David had left for Arcata, he had raised the matter of a joint checking account. I'd had no objection to coordinating our financial responsibilities for the household, so he had made arrangements for a new account.

"I guess now I'm going to have to delve into all of David's affairs, both personal and business." I looked at my friend helplessly. "Gloria, I don't even know if he has a will."

"You should probably get an attorney," she said. "I can ask Don to recommend someone, if you like."

I thought about Dirk Granville, wondering again whether I might somehow end up in an adversarial situation with him, or even with David's mother. After all, I was the widow they didn't know and probably resented.

The very last thing I wanted was a fight. It wasn't my nature, and besides, I wanted no part of David's estate. If I couldn't have him, I didn't want anything.

When I told Gloria that, she cautioned me not to act hastily. "Get a lawyer and wait until the dust settles," she said. "Don't be precipitous."

I know she meant well, but in a sense Gloria was like the reporter and Dirk, and, for all I knew, like David's mother. They were looking at the corpse like a bunch of vultures. I was mourning the loss of my husband and my newfound happiness. I didn't care about money.

Gloria offered to stay the night with me again, but I wouldn't let her. The shock had passed and I'd begun coming to terms with my pain.

As I lay in the dark that night, I thought about the troubles David and I had suffered, but they paled beside the warmth and companionship he had brought to my life. I hadn't felt a passionate love for my husband, but together we'd experienced a rebirth. What could the future possibly hold for me now, except a return to the life I'd known before—a life alone?

THERE WERE ARTICLES in the papers the next morning — one about the accident, the other a story in the business section about ComTech, the star-crossed company that had seen the deaths of both its founding partners in just over a month.

I read the stories, bleary-eyed. There was nothing I didn't already know. Nor were there any innuendos about what might be going on behind the scenes. The only reference to me was as David's widow. Dirk Granville was quoted as saying that the family was distressed at the news of David's death but that Granville Lumber would not be affected. There was no mention of the insurance policy on Robert Willis's life.

Gloria called midmorning to say that the story had appeared on a TV news broadcast the night before. She also gave me the name of a lawyer Don had recommended. Gordon Chase specialized in wills and trusts and estate planning, but was also a litigator, which Don felt might prove to be useful before matters were settled. I thought of the vultures again, but knew no one could make me fight if I didn't want to. So I called Mr. Chase's office and made an appointment for the next afternoon, determined to be in charge.

Even in my despair I was beginning to see something new in myself. They say that tragedy often strengthens a person, and I believe the loss of my husband did that for me. I found myself less willing to be led by events than I had been before.

The rest of the day I spent trying to come to terms with my widowhood. Evidence of David's existence was all around me—his clothing, his personal effects, his desk. His things were still a bit new to me, just as David had been, but the thought of having to dispose of them brought a well of emotion. Eventually I would get rid of everything except a few mementos. But I was by no means ready to begin exorcising my husband from my life.

I'd been cooped up in my apartment for hours by then. Normally that wouldn't have bothered me, but these were not normal times. I felt the need to get some fresh air, so late in the afternoon I took my raincoat and umbrella and went to the park.

The exercise and the change of scene helped me gain a sense of proportion. I started seeing evidence of the world I'd known before. David and I had walked in the park together, but I'd spent many more hours there alone. And those were the times I recalled best.

By the time I returned to my apartment building it was nearly dusk. Sprinkles of rain were starting to fall. I'd no sooner entered the foyer when Mrs. Wu, the middle-aged Chinese lady who lived with her elderly mother in the ground-floor apartment, came out her door.

"Oh, missus," she said, "so glad you've come. I think maybe somebody bad was here to see you."

"Who?"

"Some man. Very dark. I not see him so good, but he push your bell. I know you was not home and I think maybe I tell him. Then I see he trying to unlock outside door. Like burglar, maybe. I think, oh, no, better call police. They come maybe twenty minutes after he go away. Nobody dead, so why hurry, eh?"

"What happened?"

"Police say call if he come back." Mrs. Wu shook her head with disgust.

"Are you sure he rang my bell?"

"Nobody on second floor. He not ring my bell."

There were three flats in the building. The second-floor apartment had been empty for some time because of a dispute with the rent review board. Still, I didn't know Mrs. Wu well enough to judge whether there was genuine reason for anxiety or if she was seeing ghosts. I knew she was security conscious, asking, for example, that I not buzz in trick-or-treaters on Halloween.

"Well, I appreciate the warning," I told her as I started up the stairs. "You keep an eye out and so will I."

That evening Gloria and Don stopped by to see if I wanted to go to dinner with them, but I didn't. My solitude was beginning to feel comfortable again, even though my heart was aching.

A storm off the Pacific arrived that evening, and it rained all through the night. I lay awake for hours, listening to the pounding on my windowpane. I hadn't slept well since David's death, my best rest coming during my daytime naps. The nights were totally unforgiving.

Knowing the lawyer would want me to provide as much information as possible, I spent the next morning going through papers in David's desk. When I found the temporary checks for our new checking account set conspicuously by the lamp, I called the bank to find out what the balance was. David had deposited twenty-five thousand dollars in the account two days before he went to Arcata!

Sitting at David's desk, I thought how bizarre it was that I now had money I hadn't even known existed. It was almost as if he'd intended it as a form of compensation, though there was no way he could have known what would happen to him, unless, of course, he'd had a premonition he hadn't told me about.

As the afternoon wore on, it continued to rain. The bus system was unreliable enough, especially in bad weather, that I decided to take a taxi to the lawyer's office. I arrived in plenty of time for our meeting. It turned out that Mr. Chase had been held up in court and was forty-five minutes late. He was apologetic, immediately ushering me into his office.

Gordon Chase was a slender man with gray, thinning hair. He wore a bland three-piece suit and rimless glasses. He listened as I explained my situation. When I finished, he leaned back in his chair, assessing me.

"First I must find out as much as I can about your husband's financial situation," he said. "With your approval, I'll talk to ComTech's counsel. I should also speak with Mr. Granville, and perhaps with the counsel for the family. There may have been a will that existed prior to your marriage. And they may have information you don't have. Your husband seems to have...played his cards close to his vest."

"I was probably foolish not to discuss David's affairs with him," I said. "But one never anticipates this sort of thing."

"No. Unfortunately that's my experience, as well. If I may offer a word of advice, Mrs. Higson—should you have any contact with the family, confine your discussions to personal matters. Don't make any commitments regarding finances. Refer them to me if they wish to discuss settlement of the estate."

I took that as a warning of what I might expect. Still, I was determined to resolve everything as amicably as possible. "I'll keep that in mind, Mr. Chase."

Our discussion concluded, I gave the lawyer the authorizations he required and took the Muni home. It was dark by the time I reached my building. As I unlocked the outside door, I noticed that there were no lights on in Mrs. Wu's apartment.

The building seemed especially dark as I mounted the stairs. The halls, as always, were lit by the dimmest bulbs the landlord could find. I was used to it. Still, I felt a premonition, a foreboding. Perhaps it was because of Mrs. Wu and her tale of the dark stranger.

When I reached the third floor and found my door ajar, a jolt of fear went through me. I stood there, thinking, making certain in my mind I couldn't have accidentally left it that way. I was the only one who had a key—except, of course, for David.

An incredible thought went through my mind. What if he had returned! What if he'd survived and come home to me. The notion was more a hope than a conviction, yet the possibility was enough to draw me to the door.

The apartment seemed dark. I slowly pushed my way in, my breath wedged in my throat, my heart beating wildly. I don't know if the door creaked, whether I made some noise, or if it was only by chance that he turned at the exact moment I stuck my head inside. He was in my studio, the room that had also been David's office. The light on the desk was behind him, casting his face in shadow. And yet there was such certainty in my heart that I called out his name. "David?"

He turned to me, a darkly clad stranger in a heavy jacket. A cry of alarm must have passed my lips because he started toward me, marching through the dark living room, bumping a chair as he came. I spun around, heading for the stairs. So great was my panic that I tried taking them two at a time. But my heel caught and I went flying headlong down the narrow staircase.

I remember screaming, the feeling of terror, but I have no memory of my head striking a hard object. The last sensation I recall was flying through the air, that dark demon in pursuit. After that, there was nothing but darkness. Nothing.

6

MORE THAN A DAY PASSED before I regained consciousness, and it was nearly a week before I had any prolonged periods of lucidity. The way the neurologist put it, I'd had my bell rung pretty good. There was a bandage on my sprained wrist and lots of bumps and bruises over my body.

I could only give the police an inkling of what had happened, because my head was so muddled. Reality was vague those first few days.

Naturally Gloria came to see me. She was the only family I had, and she became my lifeline to the outside world. She had informed David's family of my hospitalization, and she'd even taken care of my personal affairs. Without her, I don't know what I would have done.

By the second week of my stay at the hospital my body was well on the road to recovery, but my mind was slow in returning to normal. The doctors believed there was a strong emotional aspect to my condition. Never-never land was a safer, more comfortable place to be, so I unconsciously chose to linger there.

One afternoon, as I lay in my hospital bed in a vacant sort of daydream, Gloria told me about a wonderful place down in the Carmel Valley—a sort of cross between a convalescent hospital and a rehabilitation clinic for the country-club set—that her mother had stayed in after Gloria's father had died. Since I needed a rest under the watchful eye of some caring people, she encouraged me to go there. I consented, and Gloria drove me down the day I was released from the hospital.

We stopped by my apartment to pick up some of my things. Seeing David's clothes in the closet, I experienced my first intensely emotional recollection of what had happened. "He really is dead, isn't he?"

"Yes, Allison, he is."

"Was the man who broke in that night a burglar?" I asked as I packed my case.

"They aren't sure," she told me. "Nothing was taken so far as the police were able to tell. Your valuables seemed in place. They just don't know."

It had been several hours before Mrs. Wu had found me, so there had been little prospect of catching the intruder. And by the time I was coherent enough to be of much help, it was far too late.

"I'm sure it has something to do with David's death," I told Gloria, though I couldn't say what, exactly, or why I was so certain that was true.

As we drove out of the city I realized it would be good for me to get away. I needed to regain that newfound strength I'd discovered before my fall.

The Carmel Valley is a scenic place, inland from the foggy coast and therefore sunny and pleasant much of the time, even in winter. The clinic consisted of a main building and bungalows that were spread along a creek and the lovely cypress-studded grounds of the compound.

It wasn't until after we'd arrived that Gloria told me that David's body still hadn't been recovered. I wasn't in the best condition for a memorial service, so I told Gloria to let the family know that they should go ahead without me.

After two weeks in the clinic I was practically my old self again. Each day I let David and the reality of what had happened return to my mind and heart a little more. I went through the grieving process.

At the end of the second week, Gloria and Don drove down to see me. They brought two disturbing pieces of information—one from the police, the other from my lawyer, Mr. Chase. The police had reported that Robert Willis's car had finally been recovered from the ocean and showed signs of a collision. That meant Robert had either been knocked off the cliff in an accidental crash, or he'd been forced off the road intentionally.

And in checking into David's affairs, Mr. Chase had discovered that the life-insurance policy on Robert Willis had two beneficiaries: One was Granville Lumber in the amount of two million dollars, the amount of the loan; the other beneficiary was David, also for two million dollars. Both checks had been issued by the insurance company the day before David's disappearance. Both had been cashed. Mr. Chase had been unable to find any trace of David's two million dollars.

I asked Don what it all meant. He said it was hard to say, but that the police were opening an investigation and they might wish to speak with me again.

For the next week I mulled over the disquieting news. With David's body still missing, and in light of the fact that foul play was suspected in Willis's death, I didn't have to be told the authorities were beginning to question whether my husband was in fact dead. His disappearance so soon after he'd received such a large check would make anyone wonder.

But I couldn't bring myself to believe David would have faked his death—not considering the pain it had caused me. What motive could he possibly have had? The insurance money would have still been his, whether he was alive or dead.

It seemed to me that if there was suspicion of foul play in connection with Robert Willis's death, the same could be said of David's. If no trace could be found of the two million dollars, then somebody must have taken it. To me, that was the most logical explanation. The identity of the culprit was a different matter entirely, but if anyone had a motive to want Robert Willis and David both dead, it was someone like Dirk Granville.

Of course, I wasn't ready to accuse anyone of wrongdoing, but I resented the implication that my husband might be mixed up in any funny business. Perhaps my feelings were just the blind loyalty of a wife, but who had recently known David better than I? It had been years since he'd lived in Arcata.

It was against this backdrop that I received word that Dirk Granville wanted to see me. Gloria had called with the news, since under clinic rules the only communication with the outside world was through family. She, through default, was mine.

"You're under no obligation," she said. "You can do as you wish."

My deep suspicion of David's cousin came to mind. "Did he say what he wanted?"

"I think it has to do with the fact you're David's heir. Apparently he did have a will. Mr. Chase informed me of that last week. So I guess some points will have to be negotiated regarding that, as well."

"In other words, money has come into play."

"I suppose," Gloria said. "But apparently your mother-in-law is eager to meet you. She's called me a couple of times, asking about your condition."

"Well, I should probably deal with them," I told Gloria, referring to David's family. "I'll have to do it eventually. Please tell Mr. Granville he may come and see me."

IT WAS UNSEASONABLY warm that March day when I first laid eyes on Dirk Granville. The air was pleasant and I'd gone down to a little place by the creek, not far from my bungalow, where a few benches had been placed. The gardeners had planted crocuses around the native oaks and there were daffodils scattered in beds about the grounds.

I sat listening to the birds. I watched a couple of squirrels, one scratching the damp earth at the base of a gnarled cypress tree, the other leaping from branch to branch. The world I'd been living in was a false one, I knew, but the clinic had given me a respite, and for that I was grateful.

David and I had been together for such a short time that life without him did not feel unnatural. To the contrary, I sometimes had difficulty remembering what married life had been like. Of course, I idealized the memories I had of him, but it saddened me to see how quickly I was adapting.

Yet one thing held me back and made the natural distancing process go more slowly than it otherwise would have. I was deeply bothered by the bizarre circumstances surrounding David's death. It was crucial to me to think well of him, so I refused to consider the questions that had been raised. I couldn't stop others from picking over my husband's bones, but I certainly wasn't going to be a party to it.

I was fully prepared for a struggle. Life with David had given me the courage to fight for what I wanted, and what I wanted most was to face Dirk Granville with some degree of dignity.

For the first time since my arrival at the clinic, I put on some makeup and took extra care with my hair. I decided to wear a pair of fawn wool slacks and a moss-green mohair sweater that contrasted nicely with the copper in my hair. It seemed to me that I was representing my husband, and to look as nice as I could was to do him honor. And perhaps my own pride was at stake, as well.

Dirk's arrival time had been left vague. Gloria told me he would meet with Gordon Chase, spend the night in San Francisco, then drive down to Carmel the morning of our visit. She volunteered to be with me, but I refused her generous offer. Gloria had been my mainstay, but it was time to stand on my own two feet.

I didn't see Dirk walk along the path from my bungalow. I was gazing off at the trees, my back to him, when his voice broke the tranquillity of that March day.

"Allison?" he said.

I jumped a little and turned toward the direction of the sound. Dirk's voice was deep and resonant, just as it had been on the phone, though its richness was even more apparent in real life.

He was standing at the top of the bank, three feet or so above my bench, making him seem even larger than he was. The sight was startling. He was not at all what I'd expected.

Dirk was tall and dark with riveting gray eyes. He had straight black hair that hung well past his collar, and he was dressed in a brown leather jacket that drew attention to his broad shoulders. The white silk shirt under it was open at the neck. His trousers were dark, and he wore boots.

The man's presence was remarkable, haunting, even spiritual. His lips were full and sensual, particularly the lower one. He had high cheekbones; his nose was strong and suited his exotic face. The flavor of the man was almost foreign—something I had difficulty putting my finger on. And yet the shape of his head, his jaw, his eyes—especially his eyes—seemed markedly Anglo. They were magnetic, but at the same time there was a fierceness about them. To look at him was like staring into the face of a wolf.

My mouth was agape as I calculated the possibility that this man wasn't really David's cousin. In trying to imagine what Dirk would be like, I had pictured variations of my husband—David with a provincial twist, David without a compassionate nature, David with a jocular sense of humor. But if this man wasn't Dirk Granville, then who was he?

He smiled faintly, his lip curling. "You are Allison, aren't you?"

"Yes," I managed, collecting myself.

"I'm Dirk. You were expecting me, weren't you?"

I rose to my feet, filled with awe, fear and confusion. How could this man be Dirk Granville? This was no variation of my husband, no kin of the man I'd married. I was utterly bewildered.

"You were expecting someone different," he said, laughing, virtually mocking my reaction. He descended the rock steps to the little terrace where I'd been sitting. "Didn't David tell you about me?"

I shook my head, dumbfounded. "He hardly spoke of you at all."

"Oh, my, the ultimate slight." He was looking at me with his feral eyes, gleeful, it seemed, with a sort of controlled hostility.

I found myself unable to speak. The man was so unexpectedly, so overwhelmingly different from the mental picture I'd created, that I wondered if it wasn't some sort of cruel joke.

"Well, you're much prettier than I expected," he said. "So we're even, I suppose." He studied my face for a moment. "I didn't think David had it in him."

"What's that supposed to mean?"

"I expected someone a little more . . . ordinary."

"How dare you!" I exclaimed. "We loved each other."

Dirk held his hands up in a sign of surrender. "I meant it as a compliment."

"You consider insulting my husband to be a compliment?"

He took my hands as naturally as if he owned them. "Truce," he said. "I'm not here to bicker, Allison. I'm sorry if I offended you."

I pulled my hands free, not liking the familiarity. "Just why are you here, anyway?"

Dirk Granville backed up a step, folding his arms and taking his chin in his hand contemplatively. "First, maybe you should tell me what David told you about the family," he said. "It might be easier if I know exactly what prejudices you're bringing to this conversation."

Dirk was particularly well-spoken and intelligent. That did not startle me. But I was still thoroughly astonished by his appearance and by his demeanor. His shrewdness was starting to show, and I was beginning to understand David's distrust of him. But I wasn't one to play games. I tended to be shy and reclusive by nature, but my marriage had given me the confidence to speak out.

"David didn't like you. I think he blamed you for his problems, to be honest."

Dirk laughed. "I'm not surprised. There was no love lost between us, it's true."

"So why did you ask, if you knew how he felt?"

"It was the way he presented it to you that I was curious about."

Dirk gazed at me in a way I didn't like. It was a look of defiance, but also bemusement. Talking about my husband was sport to him and I didn't appreciate it. I made no attempt to hide my feelings. "You couldn't be feeling guilty, I suppose."

His smile turned to a smirk. "I saved David's butt when he and his partner were about to go under. Is there any reason I should feel guilty about that?"

"He's paid the price for your generosity, hasn't he?" I said coldly.

"Are you suggesting it's my fault that he's disappeared?" Dirk shot back.

I was shocked by his vehemence. "I'm not suggesting anything. You asked a question and I tried to answer honestly. If you don't like what you hear, that's hardly my fault!" I was glaring at Dirk Granville so hard that my eyes filled. I would have burst into tears, but I refused to let myself. Not because of him. Not in the face of his insults. I turned away rather than let him see my emotion.

For the better part of a minute there was no sound but the chirping of the birds. Then Dirk walked around in front of me and sat on one of the benches, making me look at him. "Maybe we should start over," he said. "It was thoughtless of me to upset you the minute I arrived. I didn't come here for that. But I'll be honest, too. I didn't care for David any more than he cared for me. Our dislike was entirely mutual."

"Is that what you came to tell me?"

"No."

"Then for heaven's sake, say whatever you've come to say!"

"Well," he said, managing a smile, "for starters, welcome to the family."

I couldn't help laughing. And so did he. Yet this was no laughing matter. I went to the bench opposite him and sat down, crossing my legs and assuming a sober expression. I looked at him earnestly and waited.

"Aunt Edwina is very eager for you to come to Arcata," he began. "My charge from her is to invite you, and preferably to bring you back with me."

"I've been told that she's anxious to see me, but is it really that urgent?"

"She's convinced David is alive and believes the two of you have to prepare for his return."

I was stunned. "Are you serious?"

"She hasn't said it in so many words, but I know Aunt Edwina. I'm sure that's what she's thinking. Otherwise she'd have gone ahead with a memorial service."

"You mean she hasn't had one, because she really thinks he's alive?"

He nodded.

"Oh, my God."

Dirk said nothing. I was aghast.

"Why does she feel that way? What's her reasoning?"

"I don't know," he said. "I've thought about it, but I can't figure it out."

"Well, what do you think, Dirk? Is he alive or dead?"

He had the expression of someone who'd bumbled into an area he didn't want to be in. "This isn't a fruitful line of conversation. For either of us."

"Why?"

"Look, Allison, I'm here because of my aunt. I have to deal with her, which means I have to deal with you. It's that simple."

"I'm sorry to be such a burden," I said, seeing he wouldn't cooperate.

He smiled sardonically.

"You find that amusing?"

"You're no angel, yourself, Allison, if you'll forgive my bluntness. From what I've seen, you've taken it upon yourself to step right into David's shoes."

"What on earth are you talking about?"

"I didn't appreciate you siccing that reporter on me, for example, especially after telling her I was the one to talk to about the crime and corruption going on behind the scenes."

I blushed, understanding his hostility. "I didn't tell her that," I said. "She read into it."

"She all but suggested I was somehow behind Robert Willis's death," he said. "I don't know where she would have gotten that idea if it wasn't from you."

I turned scarlet. "That woman might have used me, but I assure you I said no such thing. Nor did I suggest it."

"Well, do you think I'm behind Willis's death?"

Dirk Granville didn't lack for nerve. Nor did he pull his punches. "I don't know you. I don't have the facts," I replied.

"You aren't answering my question."

"Does it matter what I think?"

"It matters to me."

"Why?"

Dirk's expression softened. "Because we may have to deal with one another. Perhaps for a very long time."

I wasn't sure what he meant, but I had no intention of asking for an explanation. The man had flustered me and all but dared me to call him a criminal. "With any luck, we won't have to deal with each other."

He smiled. "Here we are, at each other's throats—the last thing I wanted. One of the reasons I came was to make peace. It seems I haven't done a very good job."

The words were smooth and softly spoken, that voice of his almost caressing in its effect. But I didn't believe him. There was much more going on than he was willing to admit. I contemplated him, still unnerved by the look in his eyes, his entire persona. I tried to meet his gaze. It was very difficult.

Dirk was such an oddly compelling man, his unusual looks so distinctive, that it was hard not to be fascinated by him. No man had ever before affected me the way he did, and it made me very uncomfortable. I guess at that moment I hated Dirk Granville, yet deep inside I was already beginning to unravel. It would be a while before I knew it, but the ineluctable process had begun.

When several moments passed and I hadn't said anything, Dirk asked when I would be checking out of the clinic.

"I can leave whenever I wish," I replied. "My plan at the moment is to go this weekend."

"Why then?"

"Because that's when my friend Gloria will be free to pick me up."

"If a ride is all you need, you can return to San Francisco with me."

On the heels of what had been said, the mutual recrimination, it struck me as a rather odd suggestion. "Thank you, but I don't think that would be a very good idea."

"Why not?" he demanded. "Because I'm the hated cousin?"

His bluntness was obviously endemic. "Perhaps."

"You have no reason to hate me," he said. "Despite what you think."

I didn't say anything for a minute after that. And when the right words did come to me I had to struggle to sound confident. "I really don't see how we can be friends."

"You prefer talking through lawyers, in other words."

I hesitated for a long moment. And when I finally answered him, I spoke slowly. "I don't prefer it, no."

"Then let's put aside the innuendo and suspicion and act like two reasonable adults," Dirk said. "We've been looking at each other through David's eyes, and that won't serve either of us."

"If you can rise above your hostility toward me so easily, it's a shame you weren't able to do the same with David."

Dirk picked up a small stone and flicked it away. "The ill feelings between us went back to childhood. He hated having to come to me with hat in hand, I can assure you of that. It made him resent me bitterly."

"My impression was you were less than gracious with your help."

He gave a laugh. "I treated David in a businesslike way, and it was damned fortunate for everybody that I did. I could have been greedy. I could have demanded a piece of the action, really squeezed him. I could have wrung anything out of him I wanted. But I didn't."

"Why didn't you?"

"Because I wasn't interested in his company. I only wanted to protect Granville Lumber. And he was lucky that I did. That insurance policy saved us all."

"It was your idea?"

"Yes."

"I still don't understand," I said. "If you didn't like David, why did you help him?"

"Because Aunt Edwina wanted me to. She is a second mother to me, not to mention the fact that she is my partner. David told you the story, didn't he?"

I shook my head.

"My, he was closemouthed. Well, it's a long tale, and a sad one, better told another time. Suffice it to say our family history is complicated."

He'd managed to arouse my curiosity, and I think he knew it. David had left me in the dark, and now Dirk Granville was taking advantage of it. I found the entire situation distressing.

I uncrossed my legs and rested my hands on my knees. Dirk stared at me with those eyes, making me uncomfortable, making me wish he would leave. I couldn't exactly say his expression was malevolent—perhaps just enigmatic, like the man himself.

"All right," he said, "so you and I will deal with each other at arm's length, through intermediaries. What shall I tell my aunt?"

"About going to Arcata, you mean?"

"Yes."

"I've been wanting to meet her for a long time. Since before David and I were married, to be exact. So I'll gladly go."

"When?"

"As soon as I can arrange it."

"She'll be pleased." Dirk looked at me in a strange way then, certainly not as if I was his cousin's wife. Or perhaps that was exactly what he was seeing—his cousin's wife. In any case, I felt coveted, the object of desire. A shiver went through me. He broke eye contact and got to his feet then, as though his thoughts had upset him as much as they'd upset me. He turned his back to me, looking off across the creek at the trees. Sweeping back the flaps of his jacket, he slipped his thumbs under the waistband of his pants, resting them there. For a long time he stood that way, as though I didn't exist.

I stared at his back, drawn to him in a way I didn't quite comprehend, yet feeling repulsed at the same time. I was nearly as curious about my feelings as I was about him. Dirk Granville was playing some as-yet-undetermined role in this awful tragedy. He frightened me, but he also made me want to understand the man behind the exotic facade.

Finally he turned around to face me, his ebony hair shining in the sun. "Perhaps I should go now," he said. "There's no point in continuing this."

He climbed the steps to the path, pausing a moment at the top for a last look at me. We stared at each other. He turned away.

"Dirk, wait a minute."

He stopped, waiting.

"When I asked earlier if you thought David was dead, you sidestepped the question. But I want to know," I insisted. "Tell me what you think."

He studied me, his eyes narrowing. Then he shook his head. "I don't know. I really don't."

His words were neutral, but the mere suggestion he thought it possible David was alive sent a rush through me. Everybody had assumed my husband was dead. Now Dirk was expressing doubt about it. Oddly, I felt neither elation nor joy. I felt only fear and confusion. "How could that be possible?"

"Anything is possible."

"You're saying that until his body is recovered, we can't be sure. Is that what you mean?"

He shrugged.

"Dirk, why do you feel this way? There must be a reason."

"Maybe I just have a suspicious mind."

"Suspicious about what?"

"A couple of million dollars have disappeared right along with David," he said. Then he gave me a long, inquiring look. "I would have thought that would make you suspicious, too."

I hated him again. He was being clever. But it was more than that. I was being accused, too, in a backhanded sort of way, and I didn't appreciate it. I could see that Dirk Granville was shrewd and that I couldn't take him for granted.

He waited, watching me struggle with his challenge. "Do we have anything else to discuss?" he asked.

I knew I should say no, that I should send him on his way. But everything in my shattered life had been turned on its head. Dirk had succeeded in deepening my doubts about David. And though I resented him for it, I couldn't let things rest there. "Yes," I said, "there is something else. Are you still willing to give me a lift back to San Francisco? I can't leave things as they are. I need to get to the bottom of it."

His eyes seemed to smile at my capitulation, though his sensual mouth remained passive. "My car's in front of the main building. I'll wait for you there." With that, he turned and walked away.

7

EVEN BEFORE I GOT INTO Dirk Granville's car I was sure I'd made a terrible mistake. I packed quickly and then followed the orderly who had come for my bags to the office, all the while unsettled by my crazy decision to go off with a man I had every reason to detest.

The administrator was displeased by my hasty departure, but I gave him no choice. After my bags were in Dirk's trunk, he held open the door of his black Jaguar sedan for me, then silently got in the driver's side. It wasn't until we had passed through the clinic gate that he uttered his first words.

"You must be glad to be leaving," he said.

Glad? I felt like an impetuous fool, though I knew it did no good to be hard on myself. Besides, I rationalized, the time had come to deal with David's family. I might as well get it over with. To Dirk, though, I simply said, "Yes."

We drove along the sunny two-lane road toward the sea. Dirk was taciturn to the point of being rude. I wondered why we were doing this—imposing our hostility on one another. Was it out of a sense of obligation? Duty?

Given the fact that I was putting myself through this, I decided I might as well have something to show for it. I glanced over at Dirk with the intention of initiating a conversation, but my eye lingered on him before I spoke. I was so thoroughly taken with his looks that it was difficult to concentrate.

I traced his profile and drew a deep breath. Oddly, I discovered I was more fascinated with him as a physical being than with his relationship with my husband. But I reminded myself that David was the real focus of my attention, so I asked the question that had been troubling me for months.

"How has your aunt taken the fact that David never took me up to Arcata to meet her?" I asked.

"We've never discussed you," Dirk said rather curtly. "But Aunt Edwina's made no secret of her eagerness to meet you now."

"Yes, you said that already." I glanced out the window, feeling at odds with the world, not to mention with the man beside me. But I realized we might well go on skirting our problems for hours and accomplish nothing unless I met the situation head-on. "I am embarrassed to admit it," I began, "but David told me very little about his mother and virtually nothing about you. Could you enlighten me as to what's gone on between the two of you?"

"Isn't it enough to know we weren't friendly?"

"No, it isn't enough. Something's terribly wrong in this family and I want to know what. I believe I'm entitled to that much."

"And since David wasn't candid with you, it falls on me."

"That's right," I replied. "At the moment this family consists of you and me and Mrs. Higson. David's not here to help."

We had come to the commercial area where the valley road intersected with the Coast Highway. Dirk maneuvered the Jaguar into the right-hand lane and turned north toward Monterey and San Francisco. The traffic was much heavier, but as soon as we were settled into the flow, he glanced over at me. I was looking at him, waiting.

"The problem goes back a generation, to my parents," he began. "My father was a Native American who left the Hopi reservation to work for Granville Lumber. My mother fell in love with him and they ran off together. Before they had a chance to marry, my father was killed in an accident. Mother was forced to return to her parents in utter disgrace. I was her illegitimate little brown baby, the scar of her sin."

"But you were her child. She must have loved you."

"Oh, she did. The memories are faint, but I do have warm feelings for her. My mother was not a strong person, nor was her health good. She'd had a bad heart from infancy and her condition was exacerbated by the pregnancy. She was ill all during my early childhood and died when I was seven."

"How terrible for you," I said, feeling more compassion than I expected.

"My grandparents had already passed away by the time my mother died, which meant her interest in the family business came directly to me. So I went from being the love child of a Native American laborer, to half owner of Granville Lumber.

"I went to live with Aunt Edwina and Uncle Morris. David was old enough to resent me, not only as an intruder into his family, but as business partner in the company his mother owned and his father ran."

I felt my animosity toward him softening. "I can understand how hard that would have been for both of you," I said. I had watched Dirk as he spoke, seeing him through entirely different eyes now that I knew he was an orphaned child. "I'm sorry," I said. "I hope you weren't mistreated because of it."

"I wasn't one of David's favorite people, but my life wasn't horrible. In retrospect, I almost feel more sorry for him than I do for myself—now, I suppose, more than ever."

It was hard to tell if he meant that sincerely. I was still leery of his motives. I continued to stare at him, knowing how terribly conflicting my feelings toward him were. Did this odd attraction mean something? I didn't see how it could. Dirk was, after all, David's cousin.

We drove on the freeway through Monterey and then through Seaside and the great sand dunes that dominated the landscape on the Fort Ord military reservation. Dirk had remained silent for some minutes, and I spent the time thinking about the story he'd told, trying to assimilate it into what I knew of my husband's fractured life. Things were beginning to make sense, but I was left with the uncomfortable feeling that even with David dead, there was more I needed to know.

David. I hadn't given as much thought to him as I should have. And Dirk, after raising the possibility that my husband might still be alive, refused to discuss the issue any further. I asked myself if it could really be true, or if Dirk was tormenting me. Could he possibly have knowledge that he was refusing to share?

Thinking about it made me anxious. I again questioned why I'd come on this trip, why I'd put myself in this position. I glanced at Dirk again, feeling suspicion, but also guilt for feeling that way.

We were headed inland, toward Highway 101. San Francisco was over three hours away. It seemed like an eternity. I looked out at the rolling green hills, wishing I was someplace else. Thankfully, Dirk left me alone with my thoughts.

My mind kept coming back to the possibility that David was alive. Why did the prospect disturb me so? I should have felt joy. Could it be that I was afraid to hope or that I simply wanted it resolved, one way or the other?

We drove though the hills north of Salinas, finally coming down into the Santa Clara Valley. I tried to make myself numb, to forget about Dirk Granville and David. I wanted to remember my life the way it had been. I tried to relish the prospect of returning to my solitary existence. But Dirk wouldn't let me. He finally imposed himself on me with one of his blunt questions.

"What was it about David that made you want to marry him?" he asked.

I wanted to scream, "Because I loved him, why else?" But that would have sounded defensive, so I held my tongue for a moment before calmly replying, "Why do you think I did?"

He didn't look at me. He stared up the highway for a long time before quietly saying, "I don't know."

"Well, I won't answer your question, Dirk, because I don't like it."

"All right," he said. "Sorry I asked."

The silence became very uncomfortable, but neither of us would speak. I hated myself for getting into the car with him. Finally, in Morgan Hill, Dirk exited the freeway and pulled into a Denny's.

"Want a cup of coffee?" he asked, turning off the engine.

"I'll stretch my legs anyway."

We went inside, Dirk holding the door for me. We were shown to a booth with a view of the freeway interchange. Sitting across from him, I was again confronted with his feral eyes. This time I saw clearly the blend of his Native American father and his Anglo mother. I saw the passion and conflict their union had produced. Again I wondered.

"What was your mother like?" I asked. "She must have been a remarkable woman."

"She was," he said calmly. "Fragile, but very sensitive. She wrote a series of letters to me before she died, letters intended to be read when I was old enough to understand them. They're very beautiful, and my main connection with her. I read them regularly."

Dirk's anecdote, his tribute to his mother, was moving. There was such gentleness in his voice—love even—that I was touched. It may have been the high emotion I had been living under and the tension of the drive, or perhaps it was something else entirely. But whatever it was, tears welled in my eyes. Dirk saw them.

The exotic face across from me blurred. The waitress, two glasses of water in hand, arrived just in time to save me. Dirk ordered coffee. I did the same. The waitress went away.

"My mother was very artistic, like you," he said. "She did watercolors and ink drawings, mostly of flowers."

"How did you know I paint?" I asked.

"I checked up on you," he replied. "Aunt Edwina wanted to find out everything about you she could."

"Then it was because of her?"

"I was curious myself," he admitted with a faint smile.

The waitress returned with a coffeepot, turned over the mugs on the table, filled them and asked if we wanted anything else.

"Are you hungry?" Dirk asked me.

I shook my head. He sent the waitress away.

"What else did you find out about me?" I asked, sipping my coffee.

Dirk added a dash of cream to his coffee and stirred it. "Not a lot. Enough to be curious about how you and David got together. That's why I asked earlier why you married him."

"We cared for each other," I said, willing this time to give him an answer.

"I figured it was something like that." He smiled wryly and so did I.

I glanced around, marveling that I was sitting in Denny's in Morgan Hill with this man. "Don't you find this situation a bit strange?" I asked. "If you knew the kind of life I lived before David came along, you'd understand."

"I do know the kind of life you lived," he said, his eyes boring into mine as he took a sip of coffee.

Dirk had become intense again; the touching moment in which he'd spoken of his mother was past. In the flicker of an eye, I felt my suspicion and uncertainty return. The dark questions, even the threats I'd endured, flooded my consciousness.

"Were you the man in my apartment that night?" I asked.

"No," he replied without blinking.

"But you know about it."

"Yes, I was told what happened."

"Can you explain it?"

"I have no idea," he said.

I didn't know whether to believe him. I didn't know what to believe about anything. I felt nervous and anxious. I excused myself and went to the rest room.

Peering into the mirror, I studied my face, trying to see myself through Dirk's eyes, trying to understand his questions. I realized I was personalizing things, as women are wont to do. To Dirk, it probably came down to the simple question of money. Wasn't this just business, after all? Millions of dollars were floating around—some of it missing along with David—and the ownership and control of Granville Lumber was at stake.

Dirk and I were adversaries when you came right down to it. This trip to see me was a cat-and-mouse game. His mother might have done watercolors and written lovely letters to him, but to me he was still the man who'd had a hand in ruining my husband's life. I couldn't let myself forget that.

There was some conversation during the rest of the drive to the city, but not much. I suppose we'd gone as far as we could. But I continued to struggle with my feelings.

As we drove across town, Dirk told me he planned to stay over a day and would be returning to Arcata the next morning. "Would you care to ride up with me?" he asked. "It would save you the drive."

That was certainly true, but I'd had more than enough of Dirk Granville. He struck me as the sort of man tolerable only in small doses, at least for someone like me. I didn't handle him well. I also recognized he had a power over me. I could best neutralize that by avoiding it.

"Thank you," I said, "but I have a lot to do here. I need to confer with my attorney and I'd also like to pull myself together a little better before meeting Mrs. Higson."

"She'll be disappointed."

"I'm sorry about that. I truly am. But I have to do this my way."

He didn't argue. When we pulled up in front of my apartment, Dirk got my bags and carried them to the front door. I told him I could get them upstairs. He thought about insisting, I could tell, but in the end he didn't.

He surprised me, though, by taking my hands as we stood there. I looked into his eyes, frightened by the gesture. He held my fingers tightly.

"This has been hard for you, I know," he said. "Unfortunately I'm not very good at this. I hope it hasn't been a completely negative experience."

"No," I said, somewhat less than truthfully. "It hasn't."

"I've always been the black sheep of my family," he went on, still holding my hands. "But it *is* my family and, like you say, you're a part of it now, too. Despite what you think, I didn't hate David. And I certainly don't hate you, Allison. We'll be dealing with one another quite a bit in the coming months. I hope you'll be able to set your prejudices aside."

"I'll try," I said, surprised by his speech.

He gave a half smile, nodded and went to his car. I didn't move, watching him go. He paused before getting in, leaning on the roof of the Jaguar momentarily as he stared at me. "Telephone when you want to come up," he called out.

I nodded again and he got into the car. I watched as he drove up the street, turned the corner and disappeared.

"HOW STRANGE," GLORIA said when I told her about my drive home with Dirk. "He sounds very weird."

"*Unusual* is a better word," I said.

I'd telephoned her five minutes after I got inside. Being in the apartment bothered me more than I'd expected and I needed to talk to someone. Besides, I had to let her know I'd left the convalescent home.

"What do you suppose he's up to?" she asked.

"I've been wondering about that. He didn't discuss business, especially. His questions were more personal."

"He sounds shrewd to me," Gloria said.

"I'm thinking the same thing."

"Are you going to go to Arcata?"

"Yes, I owe it to David's mother."

"She sounds weird, too. She really thinks David is alive?"

"I guess so."

"It must be because of the money," Gloria said.

"Or maybe it's because she's a mother and wants to believe her child's not dead."

"Two million bucks," my friend said meaningfully.

I let all the implications roll through my mind. It was painful for me, because I was in a state of denial. And I was very confused, not knowing what I was hoping for. Naturally I wanted to think David was alive, but if that was true, I would have to deal with the fact that he had been willing to put me through this horror.

"David didn't have to disappear in order to keep the money," I insisted. "The two million dollars was legally his. There was no motive for him to go into hiding, or whatever it is his mother thinks he's doing. I'm sure he's dead," I said adamantly.

Gloria changed the subject. We chatted about business and matters of mutual interest. She ended the conversation by asking if I'd like to meet her for dinner. The suggestion appealed to me. I wasn't in the mood to be alone.

We met at our favorite Chinese restaurant. Gloria even brought along her notes and specifications on a couple of jobs, just in case I wanted to get back into the swing of things right away. It was almost like old times—Chinese food with my best friend, conversation about commercial design and her love life.

Don, I learned, was still very much in the picture, but earlier in the week she'd had coffee with a young architect in her building, and they had a dinner date for Saturday. The guy, Gloria told me, was too good-looking to be true. The tragedy was that she feared he might be a few years younger.

"Isn't that fashionable now, to have a younger man?" I asked.

She winced. "But Allison, by definition a man younger than me was always a baby. Now you're making me admit to being an older woman."

We laughed and looked into each other's eyes, as friends who've shared a lot do. But it wasn't the same. We both knew it. A woman simply didn't meet a man, marry and become a widow, then go back to the way things had been before, even if all that had taken place in the course of just a few months.

I took a sip from the glass of beer I'd hardly touched, then put it down. "I'm going to call her in the morning and arrange a time to visit," I said.

"David's mother?"

"Yes."

We left the restaurant together. Gloria gave me a ride home so I wouldn't have to take the Muni. While I was convalescing she'd made arrangements to have David's car brought down from Humboldt County. To save storage fees, she'd parked it in her mother's garage. Gloria had handed me the keys and told me to let her know when I wanted it so she could take me out to Seacliff to pick it up.

The car would be useful for my trip up to Arcata, saving me a bus ride. Living in the city, I'd never owned a car, though I occasionally drove other people's. Whenever Gloria had had more to drink than was safe, she would hand me the keys and I'd drive, returning her car to her the next day. But I'd never driven David's BMW sedan. He was the sort of man who automatically took the wheel.

I got out of her car and glanced up at my dark apartment building. Gloria leaned across the seat to look up at me.

"Will you be all right?"

"Yes," I told her. I thanked her for the ride and went inside.

Climbing the dimly lit staircase, I had an ominous feeling. It was the first time I'd returned home at night since my fall. I probably would have felt better if I'd truly believed that the intruder had come on a simple house burglary, but I was sure in my heart it had to do with David. I just didn't know in what way.

When I got to the third floor, my door was not ajar. But I knew it would be dark inside. My heart began tripping, though I told myself I was being silly. There was no reason anyone would wait to break in now when the place had sat empty for weeks.

I turned the key in the lock and pushed the door open. I peered into the gloom, unable to walk right in. I felt for the light switch, imagining that someone would grab my wrist and hurl me to the floor. But the light came on without anyone leaping from the shadows and seizing me.

I pushed the door all the way open. The room was empty. I went inside, bolted the door behind me, and leaned against it, smiling at my foolishness even as my heart continued pounding.

I hung my coat in the closet, noticing as I did that David's trench coat was hanging limply beside it. In my haste to leave earlier, I'd grabbed my own coat without really looking in the closet. Now I saw our coats, side by side. Pain went through me and I pushed the door shut.

For a minute or two I paced, trying to get control of my emotions. Why was I feeling this way? I was like a child who was afraid of the dark. I went to the window and looked out at the night. In the dark glass I saw my reflection, but beyond it, through it, I saw another face—one that was already emblazoned in my memory. It was Dirk Granville's.

All day long, even when I was with Gloria, Dirk had been in my thoughts. I'd felt his presence. He had infiltrated my subconscious. I'd experienced his power, his intensity, the mystery of him, and I was thoroughly fascinated. I didn't want to feel that way, but I couldn't let it go, and I hated him for it.

The telephone rang and I jumped. "My God," I muttered to myself as I made my way to the kitchen, "it's only the phone."

I flipped on the light and stepped to the counter. As I reached for the receiver I noticed a notepad lying there. There were four words scribbled in bold block letters— "WHERE IS THE MONEY?"

My eyes widened and I gasped. Who had written that? Then I realized that somebody had come into the apartment while I was gone!

I stared at the note as my skin crawled. The telephone continued to ring. I had a horrible feeling of being violated. I glanced at the door, wondering if I was truly alone, if whoever had come might still be there, hiding in my bedroom, perhaps. The ringing became insistent and I snatched the receiver from the cradle.

"Hello," I said, breathlessly.

"Allison?" came a shaky voice. It was a woman and she sounded ancient.

"Yes?"

"This is Edwina Higson, your mother-in-law."

I was doubly stunned. Overwhelmed. Everything was coming at me at once. "Mrs. Higson..." I stammered, still staring at the note. My mind was spinning.

"How very good to talk to you at last," she said. "I wish it weren't under these conditions."

"Yes," I replied, trembling. "I intended to call you in the morning."

"I'm aware of that. My nephew told me."

"I'm very sorry we haven't met before now. I wanted to . . ." I was overwhelmed with emotion, my eyes filled. It was all I could do to keep from sobbing.

"Dirk said you won't come back with him tomorrow," my mother-in-law said. "I'm so disappointed. I was hoping to see you. It's very important."

"I know it is, Mrs. Higson," I said, trying to get a grip on myself. "I'll come soon."

"But when?"

She was being insistent and I was in no mood to fight her. "I just need a few days. Say, Friday?"

"That would be nice. Tomorrow's out of the question?"

"I'm afraid it is."

"All right. Then I shall look forward to seeing you on Friday. It's not easy to find my place. Dirk suggested you drive to Arcata and telephone him. He'll meet you and bring you here."

I was looking at the words the intruder had scrawled on my notepad, undoubtedly to terrify me. "Okay, I'll do that."

"Do you have his number?"

"Yes, I believe I have it somewhere."

"Shall I give it to you again, just in case?"

"All right." There was a pencil lying on the counter near the pad. I started to reach for it, but it occurred to me the intruder might have used it. Would the police wish to check it for fingerprints? I couldn't write on the pad for the same reason. "Just a minute," I said, and rummaged through a drawer until I found something else to write with.

Edwina Higson gave me Dirk's number, which I wrote on the back of an old envelope. I thanked her and said again that she could expect me Friday.

"Dirk says you're a lovely girl," the woman said. "I'm so pleased, Allison. I always wanted a daughter. I loved David, of course, more than anyone. But it will be nice to have a daughter as well as a son."

My lower lip sagged open.

"Well, goodbye then until Friday," she croaked.

I hung up the telephone and burst into tears.

8

THE POLICE DIDN'T bother to come until the next morning. Then a man named Barnes, one of the detectives who had handled the earlier break-in, came to interview me.

"Anything missing at all?" he asked. "Did the place appear to have been searched?"

"No. The only indication that anyone had even been here was the note that was left. I haven't touched a thing."

"Had you been in this room during the day, before you went out to dinner?"

"Yes, but if the note was in the kitchen all along, I didn't see it. The only call I made was from the extension in the bedroom."

"So it's possible the note was left earlier than last evening, when you were out to dinner?" Detective Barnes, a stocky, middle-aged man, maintained a bored expression, though his questions indicated some degree of curiosity.

"I suppose it's possible," I replied. I tried to remember how thoroughly I'd looked around the kitchen after Dirk dropped me off. I recalled checking the refrigerator for spoiled food. I'd made myself a cup of soup and gotten some crackers and fixed a glass of ice water, but I couldn't remember looking around the counter by the telephone.

"Mrs. Higson, how many people have a key to your apartment?"

"Well, I do, of course. David, my husband, had one. My friend Gloria. But that's all."

"Have you mentioned this to your friend?"

"Yes, we spoke after I got home last night. I called to tell her about the note. But she didn't write it. She was in the apartment a few times while I was in Carmel. She watered my plants and got some clothes for me once, but she said she didn't notice the pad and she didn't use the phone."

"And you say the door was locked when you returned last evening?"

"Yes."

The detective went to the front door and squatted down to examine the lock. "Unfortunately this can be locked simply by pulling the door closed. It might have been picked, but there was the earlier burglary, so there's no way of telling if it was picked a second time." He stood. "If I were you, I'd get a dead bolt. Access has been gained twice, most likely the same way."

"What about the note? What does it mean?"

"You probably know the answer to that better than I do. Somebody might be messing with your mind, or maybe it's a bad practical joke. Hard to tell." He closed the door and glanced around. "Nothing was taken either time, so it seems to me like somebody's got a personal angle. A mind game. Make sense?"

I nodded.

"I don't see any reason to call in technicians. We did a thorough dusting last time to no avail." He looked at me and sort of smiled. "My advice is to get a good lock—a heavy-duty dead bolt. And call us if anything suspicious comes to your attention. On my way out I'll talk to the lady on the ground floor in case she saw or heard anything. Okay?"

I nodded again.

He opened the door, but before he left he said, "By the way, what money was the note referring to?"

The question was so smoothly put, I almost believed it was an afterthought. But the last few months had hardened me and I no longer missed such subtleties. "I imagine it's the money my husband got before he disappeared," I calmly replied.

"Oh. Why would anyone be asking you about that?"

"If I knew the answer to that, I wouldn't have called you," I replied.

He smiled at my nimbleness. "Be careful, Mrs. Higson. It's a dangerous world out there." Then he left.

The visit was hardly reassuring. I knew now that David's two million dollars had the interest of the police. Detective Barnes was already wondering about me, and whoever wrote the note apparently was, as well. But who could it have been?

I thought of Dirk Granville. I'd ask him point-blank if he'd been in my apartment the night I fell. Though I never saw the face of the intruder, I knew he was large and dark. It could have been Dirk. And the note could have been written by him, too. But why?

I thought about my husband's cousin. Breaking into my apartment did not seem like his style. And leaving the note didn't seem like him, either. No, if Dirk wanted to intimidate me, he wouldn't bother sneaking around. At least, that was the conclusion I came to.

But I simply couldn't ignore the fact that David's body hadn't been found. The police were even questioning whether Willis's death had been an accident. Two million dollars was missing. Nothing was making any sense. And I was beginning to doubt everything and everyone.

THAT AFTERNOON I had a dead bolt installed. Then I talked to Gordon Chase, who had turned up an insurance policy on David's life that had been in place for ten years. It was for twenty thousand dollars, and the beneficiary was Edwina Higson. Mr. Chase speculated that it had been purchased to cover final expenses and had probably been forgotten.

He went on to say that the policy wouldn't be paid until after a determination of death, which, in the absence of a body, was probably months away. He also informed me that negotiations with the attorneys for David's family were in abeyance pending a decree by the court that David was actually dead.

"Are they fighting us?" I asked.

"No. But you can't be ruled an heir until the death is official, so everything is on hold. Apparently the elder Mrs. Higson is not prepared to accept the fact that her son is dead, which also complicates things a bit."

"Yes," I said, "I was aware of that." I hesitated a moment, then asked, "I guess there hasn't been a trace of the two million dollars?"

"No, Mrs. Higson. All we know is that the check was cashed. My impression is that the police are looking into the matter."

"Yes, that's my impression, too."

I told Mr. Chase of my intent to visit David's mother.

"Having good relations with the family is in everyone's best interests," he said. "But of course, contact me before you make any agreements with them."

"Yes, of course."

After I hung up, I thought of the family I'd married into, especially Dirk Granville. The thing that was most annoying was that I couldn't get a fix on my feelings for him. One moment he seemed a sinister force, a threat. The next I felt obsessively fascinated with him. I couldn't seem to get that compelling mental image of him from my mind.

His brooding, sensual good looks tripped something in me that I didn't understand and felt unable to control.

I'd even dreamed about Dirk the night before. I'd been naked and he had looked me over with that half smile of his. Then I'd awakened with goosey flesh and a yearning desire. My thoughts had made me ashamed.

After the locksmith left, I went for a walk in the park. As I followed my familiar route, I realized I was neither the woman who'd strolled those paths with David, nor was I the woman who'd traversed them alone. Was that because of the tragedy I'd lived through? The blow to the head? Or was it something else?

The breeze was stiff and cool, the day somewhat overcast. There were only a few people around, but I didn't feel alone. Something, perhaps a sixth sense, made me check to see if anyone was following me. I spotted a man, but he was too far away to see plainly. He wore a dark topcoat and his hat was pulled down low over his face.

My pulse quickened. I walked faster as a jogger came along from the other direction. I turned around as he passed, taking the opportunity to look back again. The man in the topcoat was no longer there.

Stow Lake was nearby and I followed the path around it, frequently glancing back and across the water. There were other people around—women with small children, old ladies, an old man—but no one suspicious looking. Then, just before disappearing into the woods on the path leading to Concourse Drive and the museums, I caught a glimpse of the man in the topcoat again, sitting on a bench at the far end of the lake. Was he following me? Only my paranoia told me he was.

I walked briskly until I came to the Music Concourse, which I crossed to the De Young Museum. Inside, I used a pay phone to call Gloria.

"Do you have a small project you can give me?" I asked. "I need something to keep me busy until I go to Arcata."

"Good for you!" Gloria said. "Work is the best therapy."

"If you'll drop something by, maybe we can go on up to your mother's afterward so I can get David's car."

"Good idea. We can kill two birds with one stone." Gloria seemed chipper and that raised my spirits. "Have any plans for dinner?" she asked.

The question pleased me immensely. "I'm very close to being a burden," I said.

"Nonsense. We both have to eat, don't we?"

I DIDN'T SEE THE MAN in the topcoat again, though I must have looked back a hundred times on my way home. When I got to my apartment, I was intercepted by Mrs. Wu, who gave me a tedious account of her conversation with Detective Barnes.

"This house not very lucky," she said. "Maybe better I move."

"That might be a little extreme," I said. "I take it you haven't seen anyone lurking about."

She shook her head. "Now keep curtains closed all the time. Never know who take your money. Yes?"

My tragedy had upset still another life, and I felt badly about that, especially since Mrs. Wu had found me after my fall. Without her, I could have lain there for days.

"I really haven't had an opportunity to thank you for helping me when I fell," I told her. "I'm very grateful, Mrs. Wu."

She beamed proudly. "Very good luck," she said. "I Ching tell me I should go look see."

"Who?"

"I Ching. That...fortune sticks. Tell future, you know?"

"Oh, I see."

"I ask I Ching about you few times, missus." She shook her head. "I think you be very careful, please."

"You're the second person who's suggested that today. I'll be careful."

She grinned and went back into her apartment. I went upstairs, feeling the collective admonition of the police and Chinese spiritualism. Be careful, indeed.

My first act of caution was to inspect the shiny new dead bolt. There was no sign it had been tampered with, so I went inside, taking off my coat and hanging it next to David's. My second act of caution was to go to the kitchen and look for another note. There was none, so I made a pot of hot tea and reflected.

How, I wondered, had I managed to endure the last ten years sitting at my drafting table or wandering about the city with my sketch pad? Life, it now seemed, was supposed to be filled with mysterious husbands, intruders and an exotic man who refused to give me peace.

I curled up on the sofa with my sketch pad, drawing from memory. Dirk Granville's intense eyes, strong nose and sensual mouth continued to obsess me, so I committed them to paper and stared at the result until Gloria arrived. I set it aside before letting her in.

She gave me my pick of jobs and I selected one that I could complete in a day. We decided to eat before going to Seacliff to pick up David's BMW. That way, we'd only have one car to park.

Gloria had been practically starving herself so she'd be thin for her date with the architect. Except for eating Chinese with me, she'd lived on rabbit-food dinners, as Don called them. But she'd had lunch with Don that day and had ordered a sandwich out of guilt.

"I couldn't let him buy me a diet lunch so that I would be thin and desirable for another man," she explained. "So I had a huge sandwich, hating him for making me order it."

"He didn't make you, Gloria. Your guilt made you do it."

"That, and the fact that I was so damned hungry."

We laughed.

I ordered a salad so that Gloria wouldn't envy my every bite. We didn't discuss my most recent experience with the intruder, and I didn't tell her about the man in the park, having concluded it was probably innocent. But I did want her advice about the way Dirk Granville affected me. Gloria was the most experienced woman I knew, and I figured if anyone could tell me if my obsession was normal, it would be her.

Sipping a cup of decaf, she listened to my account. "What do you think?" I asked. "Is it some kind of reaction to losing David?"

"I don't think so," she replied, searching my eyes as though the answer was there. "It may be one of those situations where you totally lose yourself to someone, where they take over your soul. It's like you're a perfectly sane, rational adult and yet this person paralyzes you. You feel foolish and helpless, but you can't let go."

I nodded, amazed at Gloria's insight.

"It happened to me once. He was a lawyer, about forty. I met him at a party. He was married and told me his wife was out of town. I knew I was a fool to even talk to him, but I wound up taking him home anyway. We made mad passionate love all night. He came back the next night and we did it all over again. I don't think we said more than ten sentences to each other. He just looked at me with those magnificent gray eyes. He haunted me. Possessed me. After he left the second time, I drove to his office building and sat outside, waiting for him. It's like I had no control anymore. He owned me, body and soul."

"God, that's scary."

She sighed. "You may get to that point. Or it may manifest itself differently with you. Some people don't act on what they feel. I did."

"What finally happened?"

"I nearly drove myself crazy. The guy liked me, but not the same way. His wife came back. I sat in front of his house all night long, just staring at it. He came to my place the next day and threatened to have me arrested if I didn't back off. I almost cracked up. My mother put me on a plane for Tahiti and told me not to come back until my head was straight or I got pregnant, whichever came first. Mother is amazingly enlightened about things like that."

"How old were you?"

"Twenty-four."

"Well, I'm thirty-six. I should be able to refrain from jumping into bed with Dirk."

"But you want to, don't you?"

"*Glor*-ia."

"Don't be afraid to admit it."

"I've been a widow for less than two months . . . *if* I'm a widow. I don't think sex is very high on my agenda."

"That's what you *think*. I'm talking about what you *feel*."

"Well, I don't want to feel anything—at least not about Dirk." I paused, noting the disbelief on Gloria's face. "Okay. I admit that I fantasize about him a little. But that's normal. Even with widows. Maybe especially in widows. Now let's change the subject."

Gloria looked as if she was reading my mind. It made me uncomfortable.

"What?" I said.

"You know what's happened, don't you? David was a nice, patient, understanding guy. He brought you out of your shell, and now Dirk is the next step. He's the dark stranger who comes along at least once in every woman's life."

"Gloria, come on."

"Lust is healthy. Don't fight it, Allison. There's a lesson in this, even if nothing comes of it."

I turned scarlet, glancing around the restaurant. "Will you stop. I'm sorry I told you."

"Something to think about," she said, draining her cup.

"Thanks a lot."

"Better than lying around crying your eyes out and fearing a knock at your door, isn't it?"

That was the first thing she said that made some sense. "Perhaps there's a reason for everything," I conceded.

We drove to Seacliff. Gloria's mother was in New York, so I was spared the ordeal of socializing with her. I would drop her a card, thanking her, though. Gloria got the keys to the BMW from the house and opened the garage door.

Seeing David's four-year-old car, the one we'd ridden in the very day we'd met, sent a jolt through me. It brought back a whole reality I'd been trying to repress. And to think that car was now mine, that I would be sitting in the seat David always took, sent chills up my spine.

I took the keys from Gloria, got in, and backed into the drive. She came around to my side as I stared into the interior of the garage, so many emotions going through me, including my nagging obsession with Dirk Granville.

Gloria tapped on my window and I lowered it. "You going to be all right?" she asked.

I looked at her large dark eyes. I smelled the sea air in the light fog. I said, "I don't even know if he's married."

"Dirk?"

"Yes."

"David never told you?"

"No, and neither did Dirk."

"Hope that he isn't," my friend said.

"No, I think I'll hope that he is." I smiled at Gloria and backed into the street.

As I drove up the hill, the fog thickened. I slowed until I was barely moving. The world seemed to close in and I became disoriented and had to stop. I couldn't even see the curb. But I couldn't sit there forever, so I started out again, driving very slowly.

Suddenly something loomed up in the headlights. I slammed on the brakes and a man in a dark topcoat practically fell on the hood of the car. I screamed and he jumped back. I froze with terror, both my hands clasped to my mouth.

The man glared at me, then moved off into the fog. As he disappeared, I noticed he was walking a large dog. I sighed with relief. But the engine had died and my hand was shaking so badly I could barely turn the ignition key.

A few minutes later, as I got farther away from the water, the fog thinned and I was able to drive more normally. Arriving at my neighborhood, I was still shaking.

I had to park in the street—always a formidable task in San Francisco. I ended up two blocks away. The fog wasn't as bad in the sunset, though it was getting worse.

Mrs. Wu's lights were already out. Except for the twenty-five-watt bulbs in the entry hall and stairwell, the building was dark. I was afraid and hoped it wouldn't be like this the rest of my life.

I made it into my apartment without incident. I double-locked my door and looked around. There were no mystery notes, no evidence of unauthorized entry. I changed into my nightgown, put some soft piano music on the tape deck and curled up on the couch. My sketch pad was lying on the end table. I picked it up and looked at my drawing of Dirk.

Gloria's little anecdote had been going through my mind, and though I'd dismissed most of what she'd said, I wondered about my obsession. Gloria had always talked about how controlled I was. But my feelings for Dirk were not under control, just the opposite, whatever that was. Passion?

I closed my eyes and tried to think about sex with David. I could summon certain recollections, sensations, but emotion—apart from shyness—was hazy at best. Love? I wasn't sure I knew what the word meant anymore. A pang of piercing sadness went through me.

I stared into Dirk's eyes, the eyes created by my hand. They hypnotized me. I pictured Gloria sitting in front of that man's house at three o'clock in the morning, her heart thrashing, and I suddenly understood. I looked at Dirk's mouth and imagined kissing it. The thought made me shiver.

I hardly ever drank, but I had a craving for something just then. Besides David's Scotch there was a small bottle of cognac. I decided a few sips might be nice.

I got it out, pouring a finger into the bottom of a water glass. It was strong, burning my tongue and throat. The vapors made my eyes water, but I took another sip before putting the glass down.

The old envelope on which I'd written Dirk's phone number caught my eye. As I stared at it, I took a gulp of the cognac. It made me cough, but the warmth flowed all the way down to my stomach. Then, on an impulse, I picked up the phone and dialed Dirk's number.

I shut my eyes and pictured his face. I could feel the warmth of the liquor in my stomach. The phone stopped ringing and I heard a voice. *His* voice. He said, "Hello?" Then a moment later he said it again. "Hello?"

I started to hang up, but stopped myself. I listened for a second and said, "Dirk?"

"Yes, who is this?"

My lip trembled. "Allison," I said. "It's Allison."

"Well, good evening," he said with evident surprise.

"I hope I'm not disturbing you."

"No. . . ." He waited. So did I, still not knowing what I was doing, or why I was doing it.

"Are you all right, Allison?" he asked.

"Yes. Well, no, actually. I had a bad day. I had an intruder again last night."

"You mean somebody broke in?"

I didn't know why I was telling him this—perhaps because I needed something to say. "Yes, but it wasn't a big deal. That isn't why I called."

He waited.

"I talked to David's mother last evening. I told her I'm coming up on Friday."

"Yes, I know."

"I suppose she told you she wants me to contact you so you could take me to her house."

"Yes, we discussed that," he said.

I was operating on instinct. Words were coming from my mouth and I was hearing them for the first time, right along with Dirk. "I'm going to be very busy the next few days," I rambled on, "and I didn't want to wait until I got to Arcata to make arrangements. I thought we'd better decide now where and when you want to meet."

"It's a pretty long drive. What time will you be leaving?"

"Early."

"Figure on six hours," he said. "I'll make a point of being here from, say, two-thirty on. There's a service station at the first Arcata exit. Call me from there. My place is five minutes away. You won't have to wait long."

"All right." I'd hardly heard a word he said, I was so busy asking myself what I was doing. "Thank you," I said inanely.

"Allison, is something wrong?"

"No," I assured him. "Nothing."

"I don't believe you. I think there's something."

"Are you clairvoyant?" The words just shot out of my mouth. I was as shocked as he must have been.

"I'm not the one who broke into your apartment, if that's what this is about," he said coolly.

"It's not."

"I think it is."

"It was a courtesy call." What could I have meant by that?

He was silent.

"I'm sorry I disturbed you," I said, suddenly feeling hurt by his accusation. I could not abide his rudeness.

"You didn't. Please accept my apology if I was curt. It's been a long day. I'm tired from the drive."

"Then I'll let you get some rest."

"That isn't what I meant at all. In fact, I'm glad you phoned."

"Why is that?"

"Because I thought of you during the drive up. I was damned impolite yesterday. I said some things I shouldn't have." His change of tone caught me by surprise. "So, I hope we can put all that behind us," he went on. "I'd like to think we can be friends."

"Yes, certainly," I said.

"And, Allison . . ."

"Yes?"

There was a silence, so deep I could feel my heart beating.

"Nothing," he said after a moment. "We can talk when you get here. I don't plan to let Aunt Edwina monopolize you completely. I want to get to know you."

I closed my eyes, not knowing what to say. "Goodbye, Dirk," I finally mumbled. Then I put down the receiver without waiting to hear his reply.

9

I SPENT THE NEXT DAY working. My concentration was poor, so the project took much longer than it should have. By the time I finished, I needed some fresh air. I decided to take advantage of the car and drive to the beach.

Bundled against the chilly weather, I parked along the Great Highway and made my way across the broad beach to the smooth band of sand at the water's edge. Huge rollers thundered in, the foamy residue of each receding wave tumbling over the wet sand until the last bubble had popped.

The beach stretched in a perfectly straight line for miles in each direction, from the misty heights of Point Lobos in the north to Fort Funston in the south. There were a few scattered fishermen sitting on folding stools, staring out at the sea, their poles planted in the sand, their lines running into the grinding surf.

In the distance I could see a few strollers and a romping dog or two, but I felt isolated just the same. In a city of three-quarters of a million, I could see a dozen people at most. The darting, cawing gulls seemed much more abundant.

I looked out at the water. There was no horizon. The mists met the sea, making the beginnings of one indistinguishable from the ends of the other. There was probably a lovely sunset out there somewhere, but neither I nor San Francisco could see it.

I had walked perhaps a quarter of a mile when something made me turn around. Sure enough, there he was, a mere hundred yards away, in a dark topcoat with a hat pulled down over his eyes. It was the man I'd seen in Golden Gate Park, or someone virtually identical, at least from a distance.

He continued toward me. I held my ground, debating whether I should confront him. When it became apparent I was waiting for him, he slowed. Then, stopping, he bent over and picked up something in the sand. After examining it for a moment, he tossed it toward the water, turned and walked in the direction of the seawall. I watched until he was out of sight.

Two women in sweatsuits, with hoods pulled over their heads, jogged toward me. Just before they got to me they began walking. After they passed, I turned around and followed them, finding safety in numbers. But my eyes were on the seawall. I didn't see the man in the topcoat again, though I knew he was there somewhere. When I got to my car, I drove home.

I waited until after supper to let Gloria know I'd finished the project. I didn't tell her about my experience at the beach. I didn't want her to feel an obligation to come hold my hand. My widowhood, and the bizarre aftermath of David's disappearance, had upset her life as much as mine and I wanted to remove her burden.

"I'm leaving for Arcata early in the morning," I told her. "Why don't I drop the project by the shop on my way out of town? It'll save you a trip."

"It's out of your way to come clear downtown," she said.

"I don't mind, really."

"I'm having my hair cut later this afternoon," she announced.

"That's right, tomorrow's the architect, isn't it?"

"Yes." There was a quaver in Gloria's voice that suggested lust. "I've lost six pounds, Allison," she said triumphantly.

"You'll probably pass out before he can get you to the restaurant."

"No, I'll wait until later, when we're either at his place or mine. It's an interesting test to see what a man does with an unconscious woman."

"If I were a man, I'd be terrified of you, Gloria."

"If you want to know the truth, I think they are." She laughed. "So, are you mentally prepared for Dirk?"

"No." It was true. I was as confused as ever. I thought I'd heard something in his voice when we'd spoken on the phone, though I couldn't say what. But I was smart enough not to trust my instincts anymore.

I'd seriously considered canceling the trip, but knew I'd have to do it eventually. Besides, ominous as Dirk appeared, he seemed safe beside this man who was hounding me.

"Sometimes it's better not to be prepared," Gloria said. "There's a lot to be said for spontaneity."

I thought of the day I'd met David. If that hadn't been spontaneous, nothing was. "You're probably right."

"Try letting go, Allison," she said. "For once in your life, just let go."

I smiled sadly. Gloria, it seemed, was hard at work finding me another man.

I'd put off packing, so after getting off the phone, I gathered everything together. It had been left ambiguous as to how long I would be staying, but in my mind I was thinking the weekend would be long enough. Just in case, though, I threw in a few extra things.

Afterward, I got ready for bed, brushed my teeth, washed my face and slipped under the covers. I lay there for an hour, unable to sleep. Dirk was tormenting me. I loathed my weakness even as I hungered for him. I thought about what Gloria had said—that Dirk was the next step after David. Could she be right? I didn't want her to be, and yet I did.

Wide-awake, I listened to the siren of an emergency vehicle over on Judah Street, probably racing up to the U.C. Medical Center. Knowing I had to get some sleep, I got up and headed for the kitchen to get myself a glass of milk.

I didn't bother turning on a lamp. After I got my milk I wandered over to the window. The fog wasn't as heavy as it had been. The sidewalk was empty. I'd parked about halfway up the block on the other side of the street. By pressing my face to the window I was able to see David's BMW under a street light.

As I was about to turn away, I saw someone coming along the sidewalk from the direction of 18th. It appeared to be a man and he was in a dark topcoat and hat. When he got to my car he glanced around, as if to check for anyone watching him. My heart stopped.

He went behind the car and ducked out of sight. What was going on? A light suddenly showed under the car. I could see the thin beam on the pavement. What was he doing? Cutting the brake lines? Planting a bomb?

I ran to the phone in the kitchen and dialed 911. I explained to the operator what had happened.

"Has he broken into the car?" she asked.

"No, he seems to be under it, with a flashlight."

"Is it possible he might have lost something and is looking for it?"

"No. This man has been following me," I insisted. "He's doing something to my car."

"We'll have a patrol car there as soon as possible, but unless there's a criminal act in progress, we won't be able to pull a unit off assignment. You happened to call when a lot is going on."

I groaned. "Oh, never mind. He'll be gone before anyone comes. I'll deal with this in the morning." Then I hung up.

When I got back to the window there was no sign of the man. I watched for five more minutes and, seeing nothing, went to bed.

THE TELEPHONE RANG at dawn, awaking me. I picked up the receiver, still half asleep. "Allison?"

"Yes?"

"It's Dirk. Sorry to call so early, but I wanted to catch you before you left. I've had an emergency at the mill that will keep me tied up all day, so when you get to town, call me at Granville Lumber. My secretary will give you instructions."

I'd been in such a deep sleep that it was hard to separate this conversation from my dream. Dirk had been in that, as well. "All right," I mumbled.

"I'll see you as soon as I can, Allison. I'm sorry."

He hung up and so did I. I rubbed my face, staring at the dim light shining through the closed drapes. Why did that call seem so bizarre? Was it the confusion of my dream or was it the man who'd crawled under David's car with a flashlight? That had actually happened, hadn't it? Yes, I remembered clearly. I sat up in bed. I had to find out what that was all about.

After a quick breakfast, I got dressed. I was careful to do a good job with my face and hair, but decided to wear pants and a sweater, opting for comfort rather than worrying about first impressions.

I took my bags and headed for the car. A panel truck went by as I started up the sidewalk. At the other end of the block a car was backing out of a garage, but otherwise the street was quiet. I looked for the man in the topcoat but didn't see any sign of him.

When I got to the car, I put my bags down, knelt on the pavement and peered under the rear end of the vehicle. I saw nothing unusual, but then I didn't know what I was looking for. What did a bomb look like, and how big would it be?

Surely it was absurd to think someone would wish to kill me. What was there to gain? But the business with the flashlight had to have been for a purpose. I'd decided the police would take too long, so I would take the car to a service station.

After putting my bags in the trunk, I got in the car and slipped the key in the ignition. The engine started without a deafening explosion. Sighing, I headed downtown, trying to recall where I could find a station with a mechanic—that seemed the most logical kind of person to inspect the car.

I found one on Lombard Street. The man regarded me strangely when I told him I wanted him to look under my car, though I didn't know what for.

"Just see if you can find anything, will you?"

"Anything?"

"Something unusual. Just look, please."

The mechanic got a creeper, plopped down on his back, smiled at me and slid under the car. "Looks like the rear end of a car, lady," he said. "I don't see anything but . . . Whoa . . . Hold on."

I squatted down and peered under the car as far as I could see. "What is it?"

"You got something here, all right. Looks like some kind of electric gadget, a transmitter of some sort."

"Can you take it off?"

"It's attached to the frame with some kind of adhesive. I guess I could rip it off."

"Okay. Go ahead."

I heard a ripping sound. A moment later the mechanic came sliding out from under the car, a small metal box in his hand. He held it up. "This what you was looking for?"

"I think so."

"I'd say it's one of those homing devices that's used to track vehicles." He glanced at my license plate. "This buggy hot?"

"No," I said, "but I am. How much do I owe you?"

"Nothing. It was an experience."

"Well, then," I said, nodding toward the device, "you can keep that for a souvenir."

"Thanks."

I drove to Gloria's and left the portfolio with Karen. A few minutes later I was on the Golden Gate Bridge, wondering why the man in the topcoat wanted to keep track of me so badly. My apartment had been entered at least twice. I was being followed. Common sense told me it had to do with a couple of million dollars in insurance money, but that still didn't tell me who was interested and why.

By the time I got up past Santa Rosa, and the traffic began to thin, I began worrying about being followed. I looked in my rearview mirror constantly. There didn't seem to be a particular car that was always there, but then I hardly knew what to look for.

A couple of hours out of San Francisco I came to Willits. It was a typical small town. There were churches, a high school, a small shopping district, motels and gas stations. I stopped at a downtown café for lunch, parking right in front of the place so I could see if anybody tampered with the car while I was eating.

The town and the people seemed so wholesome, I had trouble imagining that anything could happen there, but simple logic told me whatever evil was hounding me could cross the Golden Gate as easily as I.

Recalling what I could of the tactics I'd seen in the movies and on television, I drove around the town for a while, stopping on quiet tree-shaded streets to see what vehicles passed by. I made a mental note of everything I saw, hoping I wouldn't start seeing the same car or face repeatedly.

Nothing suspicious happened, so I continued north along the Redwood Highway, keeping a vigilant eye on the rearview mirror. It wasn't until I got to Garberville that a dark brown sedan started sticking in my mind. I was sure I'd seen it in Willits. A coincidence? I didn't think so.

I watched for it, worrying that something terrible was going to happen. When I got to Humboldt Redwoods State Park I exited the highway to take the scenic drive, stopping several times at spots where there were numbers of campers. The towering redwoods seemed so peaceful and serene that I had difficulty thinking I was in danger. And yet the brown sedan kept turning up, sending my heart racing with fear.

I never got a good look at the driver, but it was obvious he was following me. I considered calling the highway patrol, but I realized I could do little more than register a vague complaint. The guy in the brown sedan hadn't really done anything. It was what he *might* do, and you couldn't have anyone arrested for that.

Returning to the highway I drove toward Eureka, discovering that my tail was becoming less careful. After a while I decided he was advertising his presence. That unnerved me. It was a bit like the note on my kitchen counter. It was meant to frighten me.

Driving through Eureka, the sedan was almost constantly in sight. I pulled over to the curb to see if he would pass, but he didn't, stopping half a block behind me. What did it mean? What should I do next? I would have tried to lose him, but I didn't know how to go about it. I certainly wasn't going on a wild high-speed chase.

While I had the car filled with gas, I studied the map and saw that the body of water I'd driven along coming into town was Humboldt Bay, where David had drowned. Eureka was so pleasant, with its Victorian mansions and redeveloped downtown, that it seemed strange to think this was where my husband's life had ended.

With the brown sedan in tow, I started down the last eight-mile stretch around Arcata Bay. My husband had grown up in this area, and I wanted the moment to be meaningful, but my tormentor wouldn't allow me that. All I could think about was my fear.

Arcata sat on the bluff above the ocean and bay, its eastern reaches spreading up the wooded slopes behind the university. As I approached it, I didn't think about David at all. Arcata was simply my destination, the place where I was expected, and where I might find safety.

It was ironic to think of Dirk Granville as my protector, but considering I'd been followed all the way from San Francisco—that I'd been watched for days and even harassed—David's cousin did offer refuge of sorts. At least I knew him. And I had no one else. That was, perhaps, the most telling point of all.

Exiting the freeway, I spotted the service station Dirk had described. As I pulled in, I was surprised to discover that the brown sedan was no longer behind me. I parked and went to the pay phone, where I dialed the number Dirk had given me.

"Please hold, Mrs. Higson," his secretary said. "Mr. Granville will be with you in a moment."

Seconds later Dirk came on the line. "Allison, are you all right?"

"Except for the fact that I was followed all the way from San Francisco and somebody installed a homing device on my car last night, I'm doing fine. How are you?" I don't know where my pluck had come from, because I was emotionally exhausted. Perhaps I was running on adrenaline.

"I've been worrying all afternoon," he said. "My secretary received a crank call a couple of hours ago that was aimed at you."

"What sort of crank call?"

"A man. He said to warn you that you couldn't hide the money forever."

I put a trembling finger to my lips. "It's David's money he's after."

"He apparently thinks you have it, or know where it is."

"But I don't," I said. "I didn't even know there was any money until Gloria told me."

Dirk said nothing.

"Hello?"

"The important thing is that you're safe," he said. "I'll be there in fifteen minutes."

"I thought you were going to be tied up."

"This takes precedence."

I hung up, not knowing for sure if he meant me, or David's money.

IN THE TWELVE MINUTES I waited for Dirk to arrive, I watched for a sign of the brown sedan, but it was nowhere to be seen. My tail had disappeared as mysteriously as it had appeared. I was still nervous, though my concern shifted from the man who'd been hounding me to the man who'd been obsessing me—Dirk Granville.

I hadn't thought about him much on the drive up, but now that Dirk was about to pick me up, a whole new set of fears took over. When I saw his Jaguar pull into the station, my heart choked as badly as if he'd been my tormentor, returning to harass me some more.

I was standing outside the phone booth, stretching my legs, when he rolled to a stop beside me. His window slid down. There was a dour expression on his exotically handsome face. I looked at Dirk and he looked at me.

He was in a cream wool shirt and dark brown leather jacket, his straight, collar-length hair shining, his eyes cutting right through me. He did not smile.

I shivered, hugging myself against the damp air, waiting for him to say something. "Why don't you get in for a minute," he finally said, "so we can talk?"

I climbed into the Jaguar. The car was filled with his tangy scent. I inhaled it as I turned to him, instantly recalling all the obsessive, erotic thoughts I'd had since we'd first met. "Hello, Dirk," I said. "Nice to see you, too."

"What's going on, Allison?"

"Is that an accusation or a question?"

"I'm not sure. Since that call came in, I haven't known what to think."

"How would you like to be in my shoes?"

Uncharacteristically, he took my hand. I looked down at it, surprised. "I've worried," he said.

I let him hold my hand. "So have I."

"You were followed all the way from San Francisco?"

I told him about the man in the park and at the beach, about the electronic device the mechanic had found and about the brown sedan. "It's clearly intimidation," I said. "But I don't know what's expected of me."

"Whoever it is wants David's money and figures you have it, or know where it is."

"That was the conclusion I came to, as well."

Dirk played with my fingers, looking at them as he did. It was a curiously affectionate, almost erotic gesture, and it aroused me. "Do you know where it is, Allison?"

Our eyes met and I shook my head. "No."

"Then somebody's causing you a lot of grief for nothing."

"My exact sentiments. But I don't know what to do about it."

"For now, there's nothing to do. Let me know if you spot this guy again. I'll keep my eyes open too." He gave my fingers a reassuring squeeze.

Dirk's expression softened and he actually smiled faintly. I withdrew my hand. "I feel better," I said.

"Everyone needs a friend."

I tried to fathom the meaning behind his words, for there seemed to be one. Dirk, I'd learned in our short acquaintance, was not one for idle patter. "You've used that word a lot since we met," I said.

The corner of his mouth bent. "Maybe it's because I like you."

There was a meaning behind those words, too, and it scared me a little.

"But Aunt Edwina is at the top of the agenda," he said. "She's waiting for you with great expectation."

"Yes. David's mother," I said. "I've hardly given her any thought, and yet she's the reason I'm here."

"She'll keep you occupied. She's very intense."

"You know," I said, smiling weakly, "I'm sort of afraid of meeting her."

Dirk took my hand again, holding it firmly. "I'll be around."

I reached for the door handle. "I guess I follow you, right?"

"Yes." He kept hold of my hand. "One other thing, Allison. It might be a good idea not to discuss your problems with Aunt Edwina . . . the guy following you and all that, I mean."

"Why?"

"She's skittish, and a little paranoid. Not that it would be a disaster, but she'd fasten on to it and it would become the topic of discussion."

"I don't want to upset her, of course," I said. "I promise I won't say anything."

"Good."

I got out of the Jaguar. When the cool damp air hit my face, I realized I'd been perspiring. It wasn't because it had been hot in the car. It was simply Dirk.

10

DIRK DROVE HIS JAGUAR through Arcata, and I followed. The highway ran along the water's edge, and in the distance I could see rocky cliffs rising from the ocean. To the east were lovely wooded ridge lines and to the west the gray-green waters of the Pacific. It was beautiful country, but more than anything I was conscious of the remoteness of the place where my husband had spent his childhood.

David had told me his mother's house was situated on the edge of a cliff, just above the sea. I had pictured it leaning against a cutting gale, the sea churning on the rocks far below. My image of the place was grim because I was afraid that Edwina would regard me as an intruder. Mothers of only sons often did that, I'd been told, and as a widow I knew I wouldn't have the comfort of David for support.

My anxiety rose as the time for meeting my mother-in-law drew nearer. Even the prospect of being followed paled beside my growing fear of Edwina. Still, I glanced in my rearview mirror from time to time. There was no sign of the brown sedan.

There was a small shopping center at the entrance to Trinidad, most of which was built on the hillside that sloped from the freeway down to the sea. But instead of heading into town, we turned onto a narrow side road.

I followed the Jaguar along a twisting lane that opened to the Pacific. The road was cut into the face of the cliff and was so narrow that only a few feet separated the pavement from a drop to the ocean. Dirk drove slowly and I stayed right on his tail. I could see why they hadn't wanted me to come on my own.

I had glimpses of waves crashing against the jagged coastline. Ahead on a point of land between the road and the ocean, I could see the suggestion of a gabled roof through the pines. Somehow I knew that was Edwina's house.

Sure enough, Dirk turned into a drive that snaked through the trees to a two-story Victorian that faced a cove on one side of the point. The woods surrounding it were dark, the only light falling on the house coming from the side that opened to the sea.

Dirk parked in a small paved area adjacent to the house. I pulled up beside him and turned off the engine. My heart was pounding and I shivered as I got out of the car.

Dirk was standing there, tall and powerfully built, his presence commanding. In the strange light of afternoon his luminous eyes seemed more unnerving than usual.

"Well, here we are," he announced unnecessarily.

I looked up at the tall Victorian. Even the porch that wrapped all the way around the front of the house was well above our heads. From the walkway, a visitor had to mount eight or ten steps to a landing, then another eight or ten to the porch. I wondered how Edwina Higson, wheelchair bound, could come and go.

The house was painted gray. The trim was white, and there were white lace curtains in the windows. The wind moaned in the trees and I shivered once more.

"Is your luggage in the trunk?" Dirk asked.

"Yes," I said. "I'll open it for you."

My hand shook as I tried to get the key in the lock. I'm sure Dirk noticed, though he said nothing. He took out my bags and, as he did, I glanced up at the house again. The severe, uncompromising face of a woman in late middle-age was peering over the railing at us. She was too young to be Edwina Higson. I turned to Dirk, the question on my lips.

"That's Mrs. Valescu," he said, grabbing my bags, "the housekeeper. She's humorless, but otherwise harmless."

I was relieved that Dirk was capable of such an observation. I wanted very much for him to be humane.

I followed him up the stairs. The woman, dressed in a black skirt and white long-sleeved blouse, waited for us on the porch. Her hair was dark, with only a few wisps of white at the temples. Dirk introduced us.

"Welcome, Mrs. Higson," she said, barely managing a smile. I noticed the trace of an accent. "I'll take those for you, Mr. Granville," she said. Dirk relinquished my bags without protest. "Madam is in the salon," she announced, and led the way inside.

Dirk paused as we entered the foyer. He took my arm and gave me a long look that I assumed was meant to be reassuring. I swallowed hard and we started toward the salon.

It was a spacious room filled with sturdy antique furniture. Edwina was seated near a large bay window in a wooden wheelchair that was as antiquated as she. She appeared surprisingly frail; her hair was white, her limbs withered. While I immediately saw some of David in her, something in her eyes was more suggestive of Dirk than her son.

Her mouth sagged without quite smiling and she said my name. "Allison."

I went over to her, taking her bony hand. "Hello, Mrs. Higson," I said. "I've been looking forward to meeting you for such a long time."

"At last," she said, her eyes shining.

We looked at each other, formulating our impressions, defining one another in relationship to David. "I'm sorry it has to be under these conditions," I murmured with a shaky voice.

Edwina seemed not to hear my words. She was busy studying me. She still had my hand. "Yes, she *is* lovely, Dirk. You were right."

I flushed, not accustomed to such compliments. Then I glanced back at Dirk, who was solemnly observing us. Edwina let go of my hand, waving her finger vaguely in his direction.

"Bring a chair, will you, Dirk, so that Allison can sit with me."

He promptly carried over an upholstered straight-back chair and put it next to her wheelchair. I sat down. Edwina took a moment more to appraise me. I sensed she disapproved of the way I was dressed and I was sorry I hadn't opted for a dress.

Dirk had returned to the other side of the room. He was standing with his arms folded over his chest, staring at us. I wished then that he had gotten a chair for himself, though I had no idea what I would have done differently with him beside me. Yet in spite of knowing that, I found myself wanting him near.

I turned to Edwina, seeing David in her narrow handsome face, her nose and mouth. Almost as if she had been reading my thoughts, she said, "We must discuss my son."

There was fervor in her eyes that indicated that she wasn't as feeble as she appeared. To the contrary, she had a power that was domineering, even coercive. Her friendliness was purposeful. It served her will.

"Aunt Edwina," Dirk interjected, "I've got some work to do at the mill. Now that Allison is safely here, I'll be going, if you don't mind."

I looked at him more desperately than I should have. Even Edwina must have noticed because she put her cold bony hand on mine, the way one did when calming a child. "If you must," she said to Dirk, "go on back."

He nodded.

"Thank you for bringing me," I said quickly. "I appreciate it."

"When shall we see you again?" Edwina asked.

"When do you want to see me?"

She still had her hand on mine. "Tonight Allison and I shall dine alone. We have much to discuss. Perhaps you can come tomorrow for supper. It's Saturday, so if you're free, come in the afternoon."

"I'll come when I can." Dirk nodded at me. "Goodbye, Allison."

I wanted to go to him to say goodbye properly, to shake his hand, to touch him. But I didn't want to make a show in front of Edwina. I feared her judgment.

Dirk left. In the ensuing silence I heard the front door open and close. A sinking feeling went through me. I turned to Edwina, who only then removed her hand from mine. A clock that I hadn't heard until then was ticking somewhere in the room. I didn't look for it. I studied the woman beside me instead.

She cleared her throat and said, "I have often envisioned this day, Allison—when I would meet the woman David was to marry. I pictured it differently, of course—before the fact rather than after—but at least it's finally happening. I'm so pleased to meet you."

I wanted to believe her, but it was very difficult for me. "I feel terrible that David was unable to bring me up here before the wedding," I told her. "If he hadn't had so many problems at the office, he would have. He wanted for me to meet you."

Edwina accepted that without comment, though I think she must have made a judgment anyway because I noted a trace of skepticism on her face. "We have a lot of time to talk," she said. "I won't overwhelm you now. Perhaps you'd like to freshen up. Elena has your room ready. I have some tea ordinarily about this time. You may wish to join me."

"Yes, I would like that."

Edwina managed to effect a sympathetic look. "You've had such a long trip, maybe you'd like to rest awhile first. It's been so long since I've made that drive, that I forget how tiring it is."

A few minutes to myself would be welcome. "I would like to rest a bit."

"Of course." She turned to the door, her ancient voice rising to summon the housekeeper. "Elena!"

The woman appeared in moments. "Madam?"

"Show Allison to her room, please. Then, at—" she glanced at the clock on the mantel "—four, we'll have tea here in the salon."

"Yes, madam."

I got up, feeling I'd been given my leave. I turned to my mother-in-law before going. "I'm so happy to be here, Mrs. Higson," I said.

"David would be pleased that we're together, Allison," she replied. "That's what counts."

I didn't reply. I followed Elena up the stairs. When we got to the second floor she stopped. "You will be alone up here, Mrs. Higson," she said. "Madam's room is on the lower floor because of the stairs."

"Where is your room?"

"When we are alone I stay in the small guest room at the end of the hallway," she said, pointing. "When there is a guest, I don't stay at the house. I'm only here at night in the event of an emergency. For the most part madam is self-sufficient. My principal duties are to clean and cook."

"I see."

"I tell you this, because madam is very proud and would not ask a guest to watch out for her. But I worry for her whenever I am away. I hope I do not offend you by sharing this."

"Not at all," I said. "But I hope you aren't leaving on my account. I have no problem with you staying in your room."

"It is madam's wish. I will leave after dinner. I didn't know if we would have another opportunity to speak."

"I understand."

We went on to my room, a large one with a bay window similar to the one in the salon, which overlooked the cove. I could see waves crashing against the rocks farther up the coast.

"Do you need anything else?" Elena asked.

I turned to her. Her expression hadn't changed from the moment I'd first seen her on the porch. "No, thank you. I'll freshen up and then lie down for a while."

"There is a private bath through there," she said, pointing. "Your cases are in the closet."

"Thank you."

The housekeeper went to the door, where she stopped. "May I ask, please—will you be staying long?"

"Only for the weekend."

"That's good. I mean no offense, but madam has not been the same since your husband's death. Her health is delicate. This visit is not wise in my opinion, but she wanted it."

Elena's candor took me by surprise. "I'll try not to be a problem," I said coolly.

The housekeeper turned and left the room, closing the door quietly behind her.

THE DRIVE HAD FATIGUED me, so, after freshening up, I rested on the bed. Edwina Higson haunted me, but someone else affected me even more strongly than my eccentric mother-in-law—Dirk Granville.

Seeing him in his own element did not give me any greater understanding of him than I'd had before. Nor did I understand my feelings toward him any better. I wasn't comfortable in this house, yet I did want to be with Dirk. How I could have let this obsession grow, I did not know. It was clear now that he was the real reason I'd come to Arcata.

I fell asleep thinking of Dirk and was immediately tormented by a dream about him. That, it seemed, had become commonplace.

Sometime later I was awakened by a knocking on my door. I sat up, thinking it was Dirk, but it was the housekeeper advising me that tea would be served in five minutes. I got up, brushed my hair and went downstairs.

Edwina was waiting in the salon. Mrs. Valescu was standing beside her, looking at me dourly. "Did you have a nice rest?" my mother-in-law asked.

"Very nice, thank you."

"Come sit and we'll have some tea," Edwina said, gesturing toward the small table where everything had been laid out.

I sat down, unused to such conventions. David's family was so formal, it made it easier to understand his alienation. For the first time I could accept his decision not

to include them in our wedding, though I would have preferred having them to hurting anyone.

"I have a treat for you," Edwina said, as Mrs. Valescu
poured the tea. She put her hand on two leather-bound
journals sitting on the corner of the table. "I have the family photo albums here so that you can see what David was
like in his early years."

"That would be interesting," I said sincerely. "I'd very
much like to see them."

While we had our tea, Edwina showed me the albums,
page by page. I looked at my husband's baby pictures,
feeling a certain emotion, though it was distant. My passion for David had dulled to the point where I no longer
felt any immediacy at all.

When we got to David's adolescent years and his dark-
headed cousin began appearing in the photos, my interest
quickened. I tried to ask questions about Dirk without
being too obvious.

"The poor little thing," I said, "to have lost his mother
so young. It must have been hard for him."

"Dirk had us," Edwina said pointedly. "My sister,
Sarah, was a troubled person and she was not well. She
loved her son, but could not fully provide for him. We gave
him what he needed—even at the expense of our family's
peace."

There was defensiveness in Edwina's tone and I didn't
wish to provoke her further. I didn't say anything more
about Dirk until we were paging through the second album and came to photos of his wedding. My mouth
dropped open as I stared at the lovely blonde in a bridal
gown standing beside him. So he was married! I'd mis-
read the situation completely.

I hoped Edwina couldn't see me color as she rambled on
about the ceremony. The wedding had taken place in San

Diego some time before Edwina had been confined to her wheelchair. She recounted the details but I was in such shock that I tuned her out. I felt miserable and a complete fool. Those vibrations between us, the awareness—had it been that one-sided? Had I been that blind?

"Dirk never spoke of his wife," I said. "She's lovely...."

I don't know what I was thinking, or even what I expected. There was no reason why he would have discussed her. Our conversations had been about David and me, and about David and him. I realized then that much of what I felt about Dirk had come from my head.

"It's such a tragic story that he hardly ever discusses her," Edwina said. "Even with me."

"Oh?"

She looked at me in surprise. "Karen was killed in a fall at their house about three years after she and Dirk were married. She was seven months pregnant at the time. The baby was lost, too."

"Oh, how horrible."

"I would have thought David told you. Dirk has had a rough life in that respect. First his father, then his mother, then his wife and baby. He's so resilient, though. That's the only way he's managed to handle it."

I stared at the photo of the newlyweds, feeling profound compassion. Just as when he'd told me the story of his childhood, I saw him with different eyes. "When did she die?"

"It's been more than ten years now. Dirk functions well, but I don't feel he's the same inside," Edwina said.

"Hasn't there been anyone else in his life?"

"If you mean a woman, I think not. He's shut that part of himself off. But of course we don't discuss it. Dirk is very kind to me, but he's never shared much of himself. Nor has my son, I might add."

Yes, David, I thought. That was why I was there. *He* was the reason we were looking at the photos, not Dirk. Yet it was Dirk who was on my mind and in my heart.

Edwina continued to page through the album. There was almost nothing of David in recent years, and there were only a few of Dirk. When we came to the last page, Edwina closed the album and looked at me. After a moment, her eyes filled.

"This is not the last chapter, you know, Allison. Your husband is not dead."

"I understand that's what you think."

"I know it's true."

I took a deep breath before speaking. "Why do you feel that way?"

"I can't tell you. It's something I intuit. And I'm very sure of it. That's one reason I wanted you here. We must plan for the future. Until David returns, you and I will be his representatives."

"Are you saying David faked his death, Mrs. Higson?"

"I don't know what happened," she said, drawing an anxious breath. "I can't explain it. But I know my son is not dead."

"Are you aware that two million dollars in insurance money is missing?" I asked.

"I've been told." She spoke quickly, giving me a penetrating look. "What did David say to you about the money?"

"Nothing. I didn't even know he would be receiving anything until afterward. I only found out when I was in the convalescent hospital."

She looked skeptical. "He said nothing to you?"

I shook my head.

Edwina wrung her bony fingers. "Well, it will all become clear in good time. David has his reasons. I'm sure he loves you very much."

"Why do you say that?"

"Because he never would have married you otherwise. I know my son, Allison."

Mrs. Valescu came to clear away the tea service. I'd hardly touched my cup. When she was gone, Edwina took my hand and held it. Her little mannerism unnerved me a bit, but I permitted it.

"I hope I haven't upset you," she said.

"I hunger for certainty," I said. "I hate things being up in the air."

"Certainly you do. I'm the same. But I know David better than you. Trust me, Allison."

I didn't want to trust her. And horrible as it was to admit, even to myself, I wasn't sure if I wanted David to be alive, either. Surely, there could be no justification for what he'd put me through. I was beginning to want my life back. I wanted to be able to go on.

"I usually rest before dinner," Edwina said. "Perhaps you would like to look around the grounds before dark. We have a lovely place here. I want you to appreciate it, because it will be yours and David's one day."

I didn't flinch at her last remark, though I easily could have.

"Go wherever you wish," she said, "but be careful of the cliffs. They can be as dangerous as they are beautiful."

Edwina Higson smiled at me with David's smile as she wheeled out of the room. She moved slowly, but surely. Her willfulness and independent spirit were evident. I had to admire her, but at the same time I was resentful of what she was doing to me over David.

I sat there for several minutes after she'd gone, then I went to find my coat. I decided to walk about the grounds and have a closer look at those cliffs.

11

OUTSIDE, THE WIND HAD stiffened and it was chilly. I pulled up the zipper of my jacket and made my way toward the point. The trees on that outcropping of rock were dense and they moaned as the wind whistled through them.

Edwina's comment that the place would be mine and David's one day had disturbed me. I wished I could go home. Majestic and beautiful as the coastline was, I did not feel comfortable here. And even if I'd made the trip in November with David, I'm not sure I would have felt differently.

It was a few hundred feet to the end of the point. Behind me, the house was barely visible through the trees. Standing at the top of the cliff, I was able to look out over the gray-green water to the horizon and a thin band of clear sky beyond the overcast. To the north I saw the village of Trinidad and the huge domed rock that rose adjacent to it. On the narrow strip of land connecting the rock to the mainland I could see the town's marina, and on the slope above it, the village itself.

A hundred feet below me the waves heaved and swelled before splashing halfway up the face of the cliff. The ocean's power was awesome and I wondered what it would be like to stand there amid the full fury of a storm.

Just then two gulls came swooping up the face of the cliff, riding the updraft until they were above me. I stared at them, squinting into a briny wind that tossed my hair and pressed against my body like an invisible hand.

Suddenly, over the roar of sea and wind, I heard a voice. I spun around to see Elena Valescu rushing toward me. Before I could move, she grabbed my arm and pulled me away.

"Mrs. Higson!" she said fiercely. "You must be careful. You could fall!"

I was so startled by her sudden appearance that I could barely speak. At first I'd thought she was rushing forward to push me off the cliff, but seeing her expression, I could tell she was concerned. I took a few breaths to calm myself. "I was just looking at the view," I said.

"I'm sorry if I startled you." The housekeeper wore a thin cardigan over her blouse. She clasped the sweater to her throat. "I came because you have a telephone call," she said.

"Who is it?"

"I don't know. A gentleman. He insisted on talking to you. I thought it may be important."

I couldn't imagine who it was, unless it was Gordon Chase. Perhaps he had some news.

I hurried back to the house. There was a telephone in a small study off the entry hall. I took the call there.

"Hello?"

There was no answer.

"Hello?" I said again.

"Mrs. Higson?" It was a gravelly voice. I did not recognize it.

"Yes?"

"I want my money," he said. "You won't get any rest until I have it."

"What money? Who is this?"

The telephone went dead.

"Hello?" I said into the receiver. "Hello?" There was no response. I hung up, a stab of anguish going through me.

I went back into the entry hall. Mrs. Valescu was standing there.

"Is everything all right?" she asked soberly.

"Yes," I said, barely managing to control my trembling body. "It was nothing."

I TRIED TO READ IN MY room until dinnertime, but I couldn't concentrate. It was all too apparent that the mysterious things going on were somehow connected with David's money. Someone thought I had it, or at least knew where it was. But who?

The police did not operate this way. And I didn't think it likely that insurance companies harassed policy holders when they suspected fraud or foul play. But whom did that leave?

I refused to accept the fact that Dirk might be involved, though there was no way I could prove he wasn't. Instead, I told myself it could be anyone who knew that two million dollars had disappeared at the time of David's death.

The uncertainty—especially of whether or not David *was* really dead—was beginning to bother me almost as much as the harassment itself. Why, when I'd been sure for so long that my husband had drowned, had I begun to doubt it now? Because of Edwina? My mother-in-law was an eccentric old woman who refused to accept facts, and she offered no proof to back up her claim. That was hardly reason for me to change my opinion.

Regardless, I was becoming more and more frightened with each incident. That plainly was what this man intended. But what did he want from me? I didn't have the money, or even any information that would be useful.

Darkness was falling. I rubbed my arms as I looked out the window, thinking what a precarious situation I was in.

I had a strong desire to see Dirk, almost a desperate desire to see him. For someone who had been alone practically her entire life, that desperation was surprising, if not confusing. It was clear I needed someone, but why had I chosen Dirk?

Mrs. Valescu knocked on my door a little before seven to announce that dinner would be in fifteen minutes. I put on the slim skirt to my navy suit and the white cashmere sweater David had given me for Christmas. I added a string of imitation pearls I'd had for years.

I looked at myself in the bathroom mirror, studying my reddish-blond curls that, despite the wind, looked better than I'd expected. I put on some lip pencil and even some mascara, though I was sure attractiveness was far less important to Edwina Higson than propriety. Still, I felt compelled to look my best.

I went downstairs a few minutes early and found the salon empty, though lit by the soft glow of two lamps at either corner of the room. Edwina apparently did not believe in bright light. I peeked into the dining room. It was lit by candles, two on the long table that was already set, and a candelabra on the sideboard. There was no one there, either.

Returning to the entry hall, I heard a door open in the back of the house somewhere, then the sound of wheels rolling on wood in the hallway. Moments later Edwina appeared. She, too, had changed for dinner.

She looked me over with obvious approval before saying, "Good evening, Allison. Don't you look lovely."

"Thank you, Mrs. Higson." I smiled. "I'm not always in casual clothes, though sometimes it seems like it."

"You're an artist, are you not? To be honest, I expected you to be even more—what's the word for it . . . bohemian?—than you actually are." We moved slowly toward the dining room. "My sister was an artist, you know," she said. "I've always respected artistic talent, but I find people in the arts so . . . delicate. The world can be a very hard place, Allison. Grit is more useful than talent, if you want my opinion." She glanced up at me as we entered the dining room. "I've watched you. You aren't a gritty person, are you?"

"Not in the conventional sense, I suppose. But courage takes many forms."

"What do you mean?"

"It wasn't easy for me to come here," I said quietly.

We'd stopped moving. She considered me. "I like your candor," she said. After a further moment of reflection, she pointed to the end of the table where there was a chair. "You're there. I'm at this end."

"Can I help you?" I asked.

"No, I prefer to do my own maneuvering whenever possible. But thank you."

I waited until her wheelchair was in place, then sat down. We were at least twenty feet apart. Edwina took her napkin. I did, as well.

"I agree that strength can take many forms," she said. "The same is true of frailty. The women in our family, for example, do not tolerate childbirth well. How about your family?"

"The same. My mother died in childbirth."

"How dreadful. With you?"

I nodded.

"Let's hope you and David have sons, then."

The comment, coming out of nowhere, was like a splash of cold water, a reminder of what I was facing in this house. But Mrs. Valescu entered with a serving cart before we could speak further. Our soup was served and the housekeeper withdrew.

I wanted to make sure the conversation went in a different direction. "Your housekeeper is foreign-born, isn't she?" I said. "Where is she from?"

"Elena is Rumanian. Her parents served King Michael before all the trouble with the communists. They went into exile along with the royal family. Elena came to this country as a young woman and worked for my parents for many years. I've kept her on. She's very loyal. Very efficient."

"She does seem conscientious," I said.

"She's always been partial to David. Loved him as though he were her own. I think she would have died for him, if necessary. I value that," Edwina said.

We ate our soup in silence. Somewhere out in the night a foghorn wailed. Edwina noticed me listening to it.

"The fog's come in," she said. "It can be such a lovely sight. Sometimes I turn off the lights and watch it creep in from the sea. It can be as moving as a beautiful sunset." She smiled wanly. "Do you like the fog, Allison?"

I shivered slightly. "Sometimes."

After the main course was served, Edwina said, "I understand you had a telephone call this afternoon, while I was napping."

"It wasn't anything important."

"Elena seemed to think you were troubled by it."

"No, that's not true, Mrs. Higson."

"You don't wish to discuss it?"

I was trapped, but in light of what Dirk had said, I decided to refuse to explain, rather than open a Pandora's box. "I don't think it's necessary."

"You're choosing to spare me," she said.

I looked at her and decided to tell the truth. "Yes, I am."

Edwina smiled David's smile. "I like your consideration, Allison. And your honesty. You see, I spoke with

Dirk this evening. I told him about your call and asked him if there was something we should be concerned about." She smiled again, this time somewhat triumphantly. "He told me about your difficulties since David's disappearance, the gentleman who's been bothering you."

I flushed. "I didn't want to upset you."

"Don't apologize, dear," Edwina said. "You attempted a kindness and, yes, I know it was at Dirk's suggestion. I scolded him for it, I assure you. I needn't be pampered, Allison. I want you to know that."

I didn't reply.

"This trouble you're having is not a matter to be taken lightly, though," she went on. "Especially considering this person knows you're here. Dirk agrees with me. I told him I thought we should have a man in the house. He agreed with that, as well. I'd hoped he'd be here to dine with us, but he couldn't get away. He's coming soon, though. I told him we would wait dessert."

My heart lifted at the news. I hoped my pleasure didn't show. If Edwina noticed, she didn't give any indication.

"I've been thinking it would be good if you and Dirk were friendly," Edwina went on. "You know about the trouble between him and David, of course. It seems to me that as wife to one and friend to the other, you could be a peacemaker. Lord knows, I was never able to succeed."

"I'll certainly do what I can," I said. I knew by saying that, I was implicitly conceding the point that David was alive; but it was easier to go along with her. But neither David nor Edwina occupied my thoughts just then. It was Dirk I was thinking about. He was coming to stay at the house! Despite my obsession, I was suddenly struck with anxiety. Was that really what I wanted? Was it wise?

Mrs. Valescu came to clear our plates as I agonized.

"I'm most anxious about David," Edwina said, "but I feel a responsibility to Dirk, too. I've worried about him since Karen died, and I think you might be able to help bring him out of his shell. Family is terribly important, and as David's wife, you're family now."

Elena Valescu was standing beside Edwina as the words were spoken. A frown momentarily crossed her face. She continued her work, but I'd caught her displeasure and wondered why she reacted as she did.

The housekeeper had scarcely finished clearing the table when we heard the sound of a vehicle. The thought that it might be Dirk quickened my pulse. I looked down the table at Edwina.

"That's probably Dirk," she said. "Elena, will you check?"

"Yes, madam." Mrs. Valescu left the room.

David's mother and I sat without speaking as we waited. I was filled with inner turmoil, buffeted by feelings of guilt, excitement, shame, anticipation.

When he appeared in the doorway, it was like the first day I'd seen him. Dirk was wonderful to behold. So quietly strong and mysterious. I'd never met anyone like him, not even in my most erotic dreams. I stared at his face in the candlelight and he stared at me until I felt my cheeks turn fiery. His eyes slid over to his aunt.

"Good evening. Sorry I couldn't make it for dinner."

"Have you eaten, dear?" Edwina asked.

"Yes, I had a bite at the mill."

"Then come sit with us. We've only just finished and are ready for our dessert."

As Dirk moved to the table I saw Mrs. Valescu behind him, her hands clasped, her expression as dour as I'd seen it. Dirk took a chair on the side of the table, midway between David's mother and me. I couldn't help staring at him. I felt helpless, scarcely able to control myself.

"Elena's made blueberry pie," Edwina said cheerfully. "It was David's favorite, you know. But then, I'm not telling you anything, am I, Allison?"

"I didn't know he was especially fond of it," I confessed.

"Really?" Edwina said. "I would have thought he'd have had you making them all the time."

I noticed a supercilious look on Mrs. Valescu's face as she left the room. I glanced at Dirk, whose mouth twitched with amusement.

"So," he said, "I understand you ladies have had an eventful day."

"It really wasn't necessary for you to come," I said, without fully understanding why. "It was only a silly phone call."

"Indeed," Edwina said, disapprovingly. She glanced at Dirk and gave him a half smile. "You know, our Allison reminds me of your mother, dear. She's delicate, yet she has courage. It must be the artistic blood." She peered up the table at me. "Is that what it is, Allison, an artist's passion?"

"I don't know," I replied, lowering my eyes. I felt them both staring at me. I sensed their questions. And I was without answers.

Dessert was served. I ate without tasting it. Dirk made polite conversation with his aunt while I sneaked an occasional glance at him, saying as little as I could. I lived in terror of Edwina noticing. I was sure I was as obvious as an adolescent girl with a crush.

We somehow got through dessert and Edwina, who seemed in high spirits, suggested coffee in the salon. Dirk moved behind her chair to roll her into the main room. As she came past me, Edwina took my hand, and I walked alongside her.

She wanted to sit in front of the fire, so Dirk and I took the two wing chairs on either side of the fireplace, facing each other. I tried to stare at the flames or to turn toward Edwina, but whenever I looked up Dirk was there, in front of me, that secret smile on his face. He knew.

Edwina was going on and on about how she and Morris and the boys used to play dominoes after dinner each evening. "It was ages ago, of course. Even though you were so much younger, you played well, Dirk. One evening we must have a game, but Allison will take David's place."

The housekeeper arrived with our coffee just then, so I was spared having to make a polite response to that. Dirk must have sensed my discomfort because he smoothly changed the subject to recent developments at the mill. Edwina seemed interested for a while, but then her attention seemed to fade. As Dirk went on, I watched his eyes. There had been an awareness between us from the first moment I'd laid eyes on him in Carmel, but with Edwina at our elbows, the tension took on a whole new dimension. I was at a loss how to deal with the situation. Never had a man affected me this way.

By the time Mrs. Valescu announced she was leaving for the evening, Edwina said she wanted to retire. I took our coffee cups to the kitchen and when I returned the clock was striking nine. Dirk was standing next to his aunt and she was patting his hand.

"I'll sleep much better knowing you're in the house," she was saying. She glanced at me. "Won't you, Allison?"

"Yes, I guess I will."

"Of course you will," Edwina said. "Now I'll leave you two to socialize a bit. Dirk, there's a lot for you to discuss with Allison. Our lives are intertwined in a new, important way," she said meaningfully. "All my children have a bright future, David included. I'm quite certain of that."

Dirk and I exchanged looks.

Saying good-night, Edwina went off in her chair, declining our offer of help. When she finally disappeared up the hallway, Dirk suggested we sit. This time I went to the rose velvet Victorian sofa, and he took the easy chair across from me.

"I don't intend to discuss business with you," he said, "my aunt notwithstanding."

"That's good," I said, relieved. "I'm hardly in the mood."

"Has it been rough being here?"

I shook my head. "Not so bad."

"She hasn't driven you crazy talking about David?"

"I'm learning to accept it as her idiosyncracy."

He contemplated me and I colored again. I looked away and when I glanced back he was still looking at me. Something about his gaze frightened me. It was so unabashed. I wanted to ask what he was thinking, why he looked at me that way, but I was afraid of his answer.

"Why didn't you tell me about your wife?" I said, my mind skipping over several steps in the conversation.

"Should I have?"

"It would have made a difference in what I thought about you."

"How so?"

That didn't sound right. "I mean, if I'd been aware, I'd have been a little more understanding."

"Of what?"

"Oh, never mind," I replied, seeing he was trying to pin me down.

"I want to know what you think," he said.

"I don't think anything. I'm just trying to get through this as best I can."

He didn't reply. I became aware of the ticking of the clock and, off in the distance, the foghorn and the faint sound of the waves crashing against the cliffs.

"Is it me, or is there something eerie about this place?" I asked.

"A little of both, I expect."

I bit my lip, feeling terribly anxious, inexplicably anxious.

"You seem to be pretty uptight," he said. "Why don't we go for a walk? The air might help calm you."

I was ready to accept, just to extricate myself from the tenseness of the moment. Then, thinking about it, I was afraid of what might happen if I were to be alone with Dirk Granville in the dark. "Thank you, but I'm really tired. Maybe I'll go to bed myself." Without waiting for him to reply, I got to my feet.

With a wary glance at him, I started for the door. Dirk grabbed my arm as I went by. "Allison, what's the matter?"

"Nothing. I just want to go to bed." Extricating myself, I hurried from the room, fairly running up the stairs. I didn't take a breath until I was safely in my room. And as I leaned against the door, my heart pounding, tears began running down my cheeks for no particular reason.

I AWOKE SOMETIME during the small hours of the morning. Moonlight was streaming into the room. The fog had dissipated and it was a new world outside. As I lay there, staring out the window, listening to the sounds of the sea, I heard a faint cry, somewhere between a moan and a whimper. It almost sounded like a cat, but I hadn't remembered seeing one around.

I heard the noise again, and thought then it might be Edwina —that perhaps something was wrong with her.

I went to the door. Opening it a crack, I looked out and saw nothing in the darkened hallway, though the sound was much more pronounced with the door open. I considered knocking on Dirk's door to ask for help, but I feared he might misinterpret my intentions. I would investigate on my own, at least enough to make sure that the old lady was all right.

I felt my way along the dark hall to the stairwell. As I started down it, I heard the sound again. A cry, a moan— it was difficult to describe—but it was definitely coming from somewhere below.

The stairs creaked faintly under the weight of my bare feet. When I paused on the last step, the soft cry came again. It was definitely emanating from the back of the house, where Edwina's room was located.

Before I could start toward her bedroom, I heard a different noise—from outside the house, on the porch. A chill went up my spine. Could it be the intruder who had been tormenting me? Or was it just the wind?

Moving through the shadows, past the entrance to the salon, I suddenly sensed a presence. A cry of terror was about to pass my lips when a hand clamped over my mouth and I was pulled hard against my assailant's body. "Allison," he whispered, "it's me."

One, two, three seconds passed before I realized the man was Dirk. He held me so that I couldn't move. Outside on the porch, I heard noise again. It sounded like footsteps, someone running.

Dirk suddenly released me. Hurrying to the front door, he threw it open and dashed outside. I trembled, unable to move. I heard Dirk on the porch and the thunder of his feet as he went down the steps.

Cold air swirled into the entry hall and I regretted not taking time to put on my bathrobe. I was still rooted to the same spot, shivering in my thin cotton nightgown, when Dirk reappeared. It was only then that I noticed he was stripped to the waist, his muscular shoulders, arms and chest gleaming in the moonlight. He locked the front door and came over to where I stood, my hands clenched under my chin, my entire body shaking.

"Are you all right?" he asked softly.

I shook my head. Dirk gathered me into his arms, holding me against his chest as he briskly rubbed my back, trying to warm me. I leaned against him, melting into his embrace. "What happened?" I murmured. "Who was that?"

"I believe it may have been your friend. A large guy. I didn't get a very good look at him. He headed down the drive. I'm not exactly dressed for a chase. And I'm not sure if he was armed."

Dirk's deep voice, even at a half whisper, was a comfort. I inhaled his scent, still burrowing against him, wanting this closeness without really thinking about what I was doing. He continued to stroke me, his touch now sparking a different sort of tremor. I kept my face pressed against his neck. "I'm sorry if I spooked him," I said. "But I heard crying. I thought there was something wrong with Edwina."

"I heard it, too, and came down to investigate. She's apparently sleeping. As I was coming back from her room, I heard a sound on the porch and noticed the shadow of someone through the front curtains. I was about to investigate when you came down the stairs. I'm sorry if I frightened you."

"You scared me to death," I mumbled. I raised my head to look at Dirk's face. "But it wasn't your fault."

"Maybe it was just as well we scared him off. He's less likely to come back."

"Was he trying to break in, do you think?"

"He seemed to be fiddling with the lock, so I assume he was trying to get in."

I started to move away, but Dirk had hold of my arms. My hands were still clasped to my chest because my gown was scant, my shoulders and arms completely bare. I could feel my nipples through the fabric as my wrists pressed against them. "Well, I suppose there's nothing more to be done," I said uncertainly.

Dirk didn't reply to that except to press his thumbs and fingers more deeply into my flesh. His eyes were too obscured in shadow for me to see their magic, but I knew it was there. I could feel his searing gaze better than I could see it. This thing that was passing between us was no longer ambiguous. Our needs seemed to coalesce. My heart both yearned for him and raced with fear.

"Dirk . . ."

He drew me slowly toward him, his grip so firm it almost hurt as he crushed me against him. He covered my mouth and I kissed him back, as hard as or harder than he kissed me. My desire turned mindless, yearning, ravenous, suddenly insatiable. I moaned and whimpered. I sank my nails into his back, wanting to tear him open, wanting him to do the same to me.

The next thing I knew he'd lifted me into his arms, without our mouths even parting. When he began carrying me toward the stairway, the kiss finally ended.

"Oh, Dirk," I whispered. But I knew there were no words that would stop him. Even if there had been, I wouldn't have had the strength to utter them. In my heart of hearts, I knew that this was what I'd wanted from the first time I'd laid eyes on him.

12

DIRK CARRIED ME TO MY room and put me down on the bed. We kissed, more desperately than before, and he sank his fingers deep into my tangled hair, hurting me a little, yet at the same time firing my desire. His hand cupped my derriere, drawing me so close that I felt his erection press against me.

His mouth began roaming about my face, his kisses covering my cheeks and temple, my eyes and nose. I drew back to look at him. "What about Edwina?"

"She's asleep," he said, scarcely pausing to answer.

"But what if she hears?"

"She won't."

"Dirk . . . I'm married to her son. This is her house."

"I don't care." He slipped his hand under the bottom of my gown and pulled it up briskly. I lifted my hips so he could get it to my waist.

"We shouldn't be doing this," I said, kissing the corner of his mouth as he kissed mine.

Dirk dragged his hand up my thigh, rotating it to the inside so that his fingers came up against my panties. I was wet. He could feel it. He knew. I squeezed my legs together, trapping his hand. Never had I been so excited.

Dirk got to his knees and peeled off my panties. Then he pulled my gown over my head and tossed it aside. I sat naked before him, my knees pressed together, my arms wrapped around them.

Dirk looked more dramatic than ever in the moonlight. His bronze skin seemed three shades darker in the faint light, and his hair was blacker than the sea at midnight. His eyes found mine as he began to unbuckle his belt. I tensed.

When he'd unfastened his pants, he got off the bed and removed them, as well as his shorts. I couldn't help staring at his penis. It was so large I shuddered, even as I wanted it in me. Even as I wanted him.

Dirk crawled back onto the bed, but instead of coming to me, as I expected, he lay on his side at my feet. I continued to hug my knees as I watched him, unsure what he intended to do next.

It seemed much too quick and it was definitely wrong, but here I was, waiting to have sex with him. Sex!

"Dirk..." I said, not knowing how to express what I was feeling.

He silently caressed my calf before leaning over to lightly kiss my toes. Tremors shot through my body as he poked the tip of his tongue into the gap between each toe. The sensation was electrifying, catching me completely off guard.

I lay back then, my heart pounding, my objections forgotten. I was overcome by the erotically sensual things he was doing to me. He sucked each toe, one after another, working his way from one foot to the other and back again.

I closed my eyes as a warm, tingling sensation ran up the insides of my legs. I'd never experienced anything remotely like this. For a moment I thought I was going to come.

"Oh, my God," I said, lifting my head to watch him work on me, "what are you doing to me?" I lay back, virtually panting, every part of my body alive. Dirk had reduced me to a throbbing nerve. I was so wired, it hurt just to be, to exist. I wanted relief. I wanted him to take me. I wanted to open my legs and let him have me. "Oh, stop, please," I begged. "Please, stop."

"Don't you like it?" he asked.

"Yes, too much. I can't stand any more."

I thought he would take me then, but instead he kissed the insides of my ankles, drawing his tongue partway up one leg before shifting to the other. He progressed this way, back and forth between my legs, painting my skin with his tongue until he reached my knees.

I spread myself wider and wider as he drew his wet tongue up my legs, starting each time at my ankle and venturing closer and closer to my center. Before Dirk was done, my legs were completely open to him. I shook with desire.

I'd never felt like this before. My body was wired, my mind focused on the insides of my thighs and every inch, every exquisite centimeter, that Dirk had stroked with his tongue. My legs were running with his juices and mine. It should have felt cold, considering the coolness of the room, but it didn't. It felt like lava pouring down my legs.

When he finally reached my nub, I jerked violently. Dirk caressed me with feathery swishes of his tongue and I writhed under him, moaning, craving, loving, hating, wanting more and more and more.

He grasped my hips and ran his tongue around and around my nub. I tensed in anticipation of my orgasm, but he stopped abruptly, leaving me at the precipice. "Oh, no. Don't stop now. Please." I wanted him. How I wanted him!

He rose to his knees, his sex protruding from the dark tangle at his groin. I reached out and took him in my hand, guiding him into me. He filled me so completely that I gasped. When I cried out, he clasped his hand over my mouth and we froze. Though I didn't move, every muscle inside me clawed at him, wanting more.

We didn't hear a sound from Edwina, so he began to thrust in earnest. I arched against him, already back on the hard edge of desire. Dirk kept his hand on my mouth as he drove faster and faster into me.

My orgasm came suddenly. I screamed into his hand, heaving against him. It was then that Dirk came, filling me, ending with a final deep thrust. He groaned softly before collapsing, and his hand slid from my mouth.

My eyes were closed. Every part of me tingled. I couldn't believe what had happened.

It was several minutes before Dirk rolled onto his side. I managed to open my eyes. He looked at me and I looked at him. Perspiration glistened on our bodies. I was too weak to move, or even to speak. I had never been so thoroughly possessed by a man, but I didn't have to tell him that. He knew.

Then, unexpectedly, Dirk got up. He leaned over and kissed the corner of my mouth and my lower lip, his face lingering near mine. It was a tender caress, and it touched me. He finally straightened, picked up his clothes and, after a final glance at me, left the room, quietly closing the door behind him.

FOR TEN MINUTES I LAY motionless. It wasn't light enough to see my skin, but if I had to guess I would have said it was bright pink. I had been ravished, thoroughly and completely. And though I was exhausted, my body was alive with sensation.

Doubts immediately set in. Why had Dirk seduced me? And why had I allowed it? I didn't want to attribute bad motives to him, but that was the first thing that came to mind. It could have been just a sexual thing—Dirk *had* wanted to conquer me—but had power and control really been what our lovemaking had been about? I knew that sexual conquest was the most elemental means a man had at his disposal, but somehow I sensed that there had been more to it than that.

In many ways, the worst part was not knowing what would happen next. When I saw Dirk in the morning would he smirk? Smile? Wink? He'd had me, so the rules had changed. I rolled my head on the pillow, ashamed of my weakness but knowing I wouldn't have denied myself the experience for anything.

Gloria would counsel that Dirk might have had me, but it was equally true that I'd had him. I could almost hear her words, "It works both ways, Allison." But I didn't believe that—not in my heart.

Maybe Dirk hadn't had ulterior motives. Maybe it wasn't just the male desire to conquer. Maybe he cared for me. I was afraid to hope, but secretly I did.

I SLEPT TILL ALMOST nine the next morning. It was a sunny day, though there were broken clouds in the sky. Immediately I recalled the night before, and a rush of anguish overwhelmed me.

I got up and, seeing my nightgown, quickly put it on. I went to the window and looked out at the cove. The churning sea was unchanged, but that wasn't true of me. I had been transformed.

I had my usual desire to run from the problem. I might even have gotten in my car and taken off, if it could have been done easily. But it couldn't be done easily, and I knew I'd have to face the music eventually. Best I get downstairs and get it over with.

I showered and dressed as if I was going to church. The silk blouse I wore had long sleeves and buttoned to the neck. I added a gold chain, my navy skirt and pumps. I was jittery, worse even than the day I'd married David.

Both Edwina and Dirk were in the dining room. They were drinking coffee and chatting. Appearing in the doorway, I waited until Dirk noticed me, then I turned to my mother-in-law.

"Good morning, my dear," she said, again approving of my dress.

"I'm sorry to have slept in. I don't know why I... I guess I was tired." I went to my place without looking at Dirk. I took my napkin and smoothed it on my lap, certain that I was crimson. My ears burned, but I managed to meet Edwina's serene, contented gaze. I realized then that she didn't know. There wasn't the slightest sign of suspicion on her face.

"We had a late breakfast, too," Dirk said amiably.

I gave him a cursory glance and smiled. I still hadn't looked at him long enough to draw any conclusions about his state of mind, but my instincts told me he was acting as though nothing had happened. That was a relief.

"Are you hungry, Allison?" Edwina asked. "Elena can make whatever you wish."

The housekeeper appeared just then with the coffee-pot. I asked for scrambled eggs and toast. I did watch Mrs. Valescu carefully, finding her as harsh in demeanor as the day before, and disapproving. My guilt served to amplify my feelings, and I decided the woman didn't like me any more than I liked her.

When the three of us were alone, Edwina said, "Dirk told me what happened last night, Allison."

I looked up in utter horror.

"Something must be done about that dreadful man," she went on. "I insisted Dirk talk to the police. I won't have my own daughter-in-law harassed while she's in my house. I simply won't."

The relief on my face must have bordered on the comical because I saw Dirk smile. I managed to give him a look without Edwina noticing, which amused him even more. The exchange did lessen the tension some, however.

"I talked to the sheriff this morning," Dirk said, managing to sound as innocent as a babe. "I informed him about the car that followed you. Without a more detailed description there's not a lot they can do, but they've agreed to watch the road at night. There won't be many brown sedans running around here at two in the morning, so if the guy ventures back, he may be in for trouble."

I watched Dirk the whole time he spoke, my eyes fixed on the mouth that had kissed me. I was acutely aware of our secret, and I flushed as snippets of the night before went through my mind. But Dirk was cool, even in the presence of Edwina.

"Maybe they'll catch him and I won't have to deal with him following me back to San Francisco," I said, knowing I had to say something.

"We certainly don't need the distraction," Edwina agreed. She sipped her coffee. "I've been thinking about David," she went on, as though he was the logical extension of her thought, "and I've decided that something should be done about finances before he returns. I'm going to meet with our attorney this afternoon. He's been good enough to agree to see me even though it's Saturday. We're going to discuss how you fit into the family interests. Then on Monday perhaps you can meet with him yourself, Allison, and we can begin making plans."

I wasn't quite sure what she had in mind, but I wasn't prepared to question her. "If you wish."

"In the meantime I want you to enjoy yourself," she said. "I've charged Dirk with the responsibility of acquainting you with our lives here—the town, our business, everything. It was once David's life and it will be again."

I winced at her references to David, as though any day he would be returning from a business trip. Before, I'd dismissed it as the old lady's eccentricity, but after making love with Dirk, I didn't want to be reminded that my husband's death had not been confirmed.

Edwina continued on and as she did, I happened to notice a crack in the swing door to the kitchen. Mrs. Valescu was listening. When she noticed me eyeing the door, she let it slip shut.

"As for today," Edwina was saying, "I've suggested to Dirk that he show you our little cove, so you can get a feel for our home here. The boys played on the beach growing up, and Morris and I used to enjoy walking down there. If you want a picnic, I'll have Elena make one. You should make it a real outing," she said with a smile. "The air will be good for you."

I groaned to myself, thinking if she knew the truth, Dirk and I would be drawn and quartered. I glanced his way and found him still swaddled in an expression of innocence. Didn't the man have a conscience?

"Dirk suggested he take us both out to dinner this evening since I hardly ever leave the house," Edwina continued, "but I told him there was good reason I didn't venture out. So he will be taking you alone, Allison. I suggested the village, but if you'd rather drive into Arcata or Eureka, that's your business."

I looked at Dirk again. He sat impassively. It made me want to swat him, but at the same time I was grateful. He could have been much worse. Of course, it remained to be seen how he would act once we were alone.

After I'd eaten, and we'd all had a final cup of coffee, Edwina excused herself to tend to some correspondence. Mrs. Valescu came to clear away the dishes and Dirk suggested we retire to the salon.

We left the dining room together. I tensed when he touched my arm, but neither of us spoke. For some reason—cowardice, perhaps—I couldn't just sit down in a chair and face him, so I went to the window to gaze at the seascape. Dirk was somewhere behind me, I didn't know where. For the moment I ignored him.

"Do you want to discuss plans for the day?" he said after a while.

My anxiety boiled up in a flash of temper. I spun around to face him. "Don't you think plans for the future are a little more appropriate?" I'd kept my voice low, but there was enough emotion in it that Dirk glanced over his shoulder, toward the door.

"You're upset with me," he said calmly.

I wrung my hands. "Not upset, exactly. Confused is more like it."

Dirk came closer. He gave me a long, penetrating look. I stared at his mouth. I thought of his tongue, his naked body, his strength. I shivered and looked away. He touched my arm and I froze.

"What have we done?" I said with a quavering voice.

"I think that's pretty plain. The question is how you feel about it."

"I feel dreadful," I snapped.

"You didn't like it?" His voice mocked me.

I glanced over his shoulder toward the door, lowering my voice to a whisper. "Of course I *liked* it. But that isn't the issue."

"It seems to me it is."

"Well, maybe that's because that's the way you're made, but I don't go around jumping into bed with whoever comes along."

"I don't recall saying you did."

"You didn't."

"Well?"

I took an angry breath. "Last night you acted as though you had every right to do with me exactly what you wanted."

"I don't recall any protest from you," he shot back.

"No," I said. "I let the moment overwhelm me. So I'm to blame, as well."

"Then why are you so angry?"

"Because it never should have happened!" I hissed.

Now it was Dirk's turn to draw an indignant breath. "I didn't plan it," he said after a moment.

"Then why did you do it?"

He looked me dead in the eye. "Because I wanted to. Maybe I wanted to from the first day I saw you. And your reaction told me you wanted the same thing."

I opened my mouth, poised to reply, when Elena Valescu appeared. "Excuse me, Mr. Granville," the housekeeper said in her thick accent, "but madam told me you and Mrs. Higson wish a picnic lunch. What shall I fix for you?"

"I'm not so sure it's necessary, Mrs. Valescu," I said, moving a step or two away from Dirk.

"Yes, it is," he countered. "What kind of sandwich can you make us?"

"Whatever you wish, sir. I have roast beef, ham, cheese, tuna. I can make egg salad or chicken salad. Whatever you wish."

"Allison," Dirk said to me, "what do you want?"

I glared at him, but not too obviously. "Roast beef, I suppose."

"On wheat bread?"

I sighed impatiently. "Yes."

"I'll have the same," Dirk said. "One sandwich each is enough. Throw some other things in the basket. The ocean air always makes you hungrier than you expect."

"Yes, Mr. Granville." Mrs. Valescu bowed slightly and left the room, walking off in her stiff gait.

When she was gone, Dirk and I looked at each other. The tension between us was rife.

"I think we need to avoid seeming hostile toward each other," he said, striving for a more accommodating tone. "Aunt Edwina is so wrapped up in her plans that she's a bit oblivious. Elena, on the other hand, has the mind of a Nazi storm trooper. We have to be careful around her."

"Maybe the danger wouldn't be so great if you went away," I said as calmly as I could. "Being around each other is inviting trouble."

He smiled. It was actually a warm smile. "I guess I like living dangerously." He lowered his voice. "Tonight, right after dinner, we'll go to my place. We'll be able to relax a little more there."

I couldn't believe it! He was telling me he planned to make love to me again! "That's not a good idea," I stammered.

"Do you have a better one?"

I was at a loss. During the entire conversation my words had been in direct conflict with my true feelings. All I could do was groan.

Dirk took a precautionary glance in the direction of the doorway, then reached out and caressed my cheek. "You'll want to change. You can't go to the beach like that."

"You really expect me to go with you."

"You wouldn't want to disappoint Aunt Edwina, would you?"

I stomped off, fairly running up the stairs to my room. For a minute I paced back and forth. Then I went to the closet and took out a warm sweater and a pair of jeans.

13

DIRK WAS WAITING FOR me in the entry hall with a picnic basket and a blanket. He was wearing a gray sweatshirt and faded jeans. Seeing him look up at me expectantly, happily, I wondered for the first time if it was possible I was falling in love with him.

There was no doubting the fact I'd been obsessed with him from the first. Maybe Dirk felt the same. He'd said he'd wanted me even then. But wanting and being obsessed were not quite the same as loving. Love was different; and the thought that went through my mind when I saw his face wasn't about desire or sex, it was about love.

"Ready?" he asked chipperly.

My suspicions and guilt and fear seemed miraculously to have vanished. I was buoyant and eager. How could my feelings alter so quickly?

We put on our jackets, then went out the front door and down the steps. As we headed toward the path that led to the cove, Dirk took my hand. I happened to glance back at the house just then. Standing in the big bay window of the salon, I saw Mrs. Valescu. She was too far away for me to see her expression, but I had no doubt it was grim.

As we clambered down the steep slope I told Dirk I'd seen her watching us.

"Don't worry about her," he said, taking hold of the rough-hewn railing. "I've survived pretty well without her friendship. You will, too."

The last section of the path was very steep and ran straight down the slope, ending on the sandy beach. Dirk let go of my hand just before he ran down it, so as not to have to worry about slipping. He put down the basket and blanket and signaled for me to follow.

I was never very athletic, but something about Dirk Granville gave me courage. Lord knows, he'd inspired me to let go of my inhibitions and act with abandon the night before.

Taking a deep breath, I started down the slope, taking baby steps at first, and then larger and larger ones as my momentum built. By the time I reached the bottom I was almost running. I would have plunged headlong into the sand except that Dirk caught me. I ended up in his arms, my body pressed against his chest.

I was laughing with excitement and so was he. Our faces were only inches apart. Then something happened. It was as if at the same moment we both remembered. He kissed me. At first he was tender, signaling his remembrance. But then our passion grew and the kiss became more frantic.

Whatever control I had was instantly gone. After a minute I forced my mouth free so I could breathe, but my body was already humming with that same uncompromising desire.

"My God," I said, "how do you manage to excite me so easily?"

"Just lucky, I guess." He kissed me again.

Even though I was weak in the knees I forced him away. "We can't. Someone might see." I peered up the face of the cliff, expecting to see Mrs. Valescu again, but she wasn't there. I took another breath to calm myself.

"There's something about you, Allison, that makes me lose control."

The wind had blown my hair across my face and I brushed it back. "I can see that."

He was smiling.

"But try to be a gentleman. Please."

He picked up the basket and blanket. "I'll do my best."

Dirk showed me a little grotto that time had carved into the face of the cliff. It had been his hideout as a child. We left our things there and strolled along the small beach that ringed the cove. We walked side by side.

I glanced around, trying to get a sense of the place, which was, after all, the reason he'd supposedly brought me there. I gazed out at the rollers coming in from the sea. From ground level they seemed enormous, but mostly they broke up on the rocks at the outer edge of the cove, their fury spent by the time they reached the beach.

I kept my face to the wind so that my hair stayed out of my eyes. Whenever I turned toward Dirk, I had to hold it back with my hand. He moved to the other side of me to eliminate the problem.

"It's a damned shame I can't kiss you," he said. "Because I'd really like to."

"I wish you wouldn't say things like that."

He chuckled. "Does it offend you?"

"No. It makes me think," I said. "And I don't want to think just yet."

He was quiet for a long moment. "Yes, you're right. There'll be plenty of time for that later. A lot more than we'll want, probably." It was the first time he'd acknowledged, even indirectly, that we'd be facing major problems down the road.

"Tell me about your wife," I said on an impulse. "What was she like?"

He didn't seem pleased by the question, but he must have understood my curiosity because he answered. "She was gentle. Quiet. Shy. We met when I went with a friend of mine to his kid's graduation from kindergarten. Karen was the teacher. Obviously she liked children. When she found out she was pregnant she was just ecstatic."

I could see his eyes glistening with emotion. "You must have loved her very much."

"I did."

We came to the far end of the little beach and Dirk sat on a rock, staring out to sea. I sat next to him, and we pondered the ocean and the gulls.

"Have there been many women since she died?" I asked.

He contemplated me for a moment before his lips bent wryly. He seemed amused. "Why? Do you want to know if what happened last night occurs all the time?"

"I don't know if I'd phrase it that way, but I am curious why you picked me."

"Why shouldn't I?"

"Was it because I'm married to David?"

He did not look pleased. "You think he's the reason I want you, Allison?"

"I don't know."

"Did you want me?" he asked.

"Yes."

"Then it's fairly obvious why it happened, isn't it?"

"I guess I know why *I* did it," I said, waiting.

He casually put his hand on my arm, so subtly that someone watching from afar wouldn't notice. "My reason is probably the same as yours," he said. "I couldn't help myself. I had to have you."

I grinned and Dirk peered at me with his dark, mysterious eyes. I watched his black hair being tossed about by the wind. I remembered him naked in my bed.

"You're smiling," he said.

"I'm still not sure it really happened."

"It did."

I shook my head.

"Why don't you want to believe it?"

"If you knew how unlikely it is that a man would be lusting after me . . . that I would be having an affair only months after marrying someone else, you'd laugh, Dirk. You'd laugh out loud."

"What am I hearing?" he asked. "That you were a virgin bride?"

"Not quite, but almost."

"I don't see what that has to do with anything. So what?"

I took a handful of my hair and held it behind my head as I squinted into the briny wind. "I guess I'm trying to understand a few things. I'm not the same person I was a year ago."

"I didn't know you a year ago."

"Trust me," I said.

Dirk smiled gently. "Then I wouldn't have felt this way a year ago."

I wasn't sure what he meant, but for the moment I was willing to accept the fact that somehow, in some way, for some reason, Dirk Granville wanted me now.

We headed back to the grotto. Dirk spread the blanket in the sand and lay down in the middle of it, inviting me to join him. I lay next to him, propped up on my elbow, still in awe of everything that happened since he'd carried me up the stairs. I had a lot of natural skepticism to overcome.

Dirk stroked my cheek.

"Is David dead?" I asked. The question just popped out of me. "When I came up here, I was sure he was. Now I'm beginning to have doubts."

"You asked me that once already, remember?"

"Yes, but I want to know what you're thinking now."

"Does it make any difference whether or not he's alive?" Dirk asked.

"Of course it does. I'm either a widow or I'm not."

"I meant, does it make any difference in the way you feel about me?"

I drew an uneasy breath. "I don't even know what the right answer is to a question like that."

"The *right* answer doesn't matter," he said. "It's *your* answer I care about."

"I don't know," I said honestly, searching his eyes.

"Let's say I told you he was alive. Would that change what happens tonight or the night after?"

It was an obvious question, yet one I hadn't fully considered. When the possibility that David was alive first occurred to me, back in Carmel, I wasn't sure whether I could ever live with him again—pretending that nothing had happened. How could I possibly have known how I'd feel, when I hadn't heard his side of the story? But that had been before Dirk. Before last night.

I looked at Dirk questioningly. "You aren't suggesting that you know about David, are you?"

He shook his head. "I just want to make sure how you feel."

"I feel guilty."

He rolled onto his side, bringing his face right up against mine. I could smell him right along with the sand and the sea. Even the taste of him had become familiar. He lightly kissed my lower lip and the tip of my nose.

"For two cents I'd make love with you right here, right now," he said.

I kissed his chin. "I wouldn't let you."

"You let me last night."

"But this is different," I insisted.

Dirk slipped his hand under my sweater. I trembled at the feel of it. He ran his hand over my back, and began fiddling with my bra strap.

"Don't do that," I admonished. But it was too late. He already had the hook undone and was cupping my breast. "Dirk!" I tried to pull away, but he drew me down on top of him, kissing me deeply.

That yearning ache returned. I felt myself moisten. Knowing we shouldn't be doing this, I yanked my mouth free.

"Stop," I commanded.

Dirk let his head fall back on the blanket and he closed his eyes. I looked down at the bulge in his jeans. I wasn't the only one who got excited easily.

"We're worse than a couple of kids," I said.

"Yes. Wonderful to grow young again, isn't it?"

"It's not funny."

He sighed and I sat up to refasten my bra, glancing out at the beach as I did so. Something caught my eye on top of the cliff halfway around the cove. It was a car, and a woman was standing next to it. I couldn't tell who; it was too far away.

"Dirk," I said, "someone's watching us."

He rose to his elbows and looked to where I pointed. The woman promptly got in the car and drove away. We were able to see her for a distance before the vehicle disappeared around a bend.

"Who do you suppose that was?" I asked.

"Elena Valescu," he replied. "I recognized the car."

"Oh, my God. Do you think she'll tell Edwina?"

"Tell her what?"

"That we were lying on the blanket together and kissing, of course. What do you think?"

Dirk seemed surprisingly unperturbed. "Somehow I don't think so."

"Why not?"

"There's nothing to be gained. I've never taken Elena very seriously."

I regarded him, deciding he was being honest. After all, there was no reason for him to lie. But I couldn't help thinking he was taking the woman too lightly. Something told me she was up to something. I just had no way of knowing what.

WE RETURNED TO THE HOUSE in midafternoon. Mrs. Valescu's car, the one we'd seen on the road, was back in the garage. She apparently had returned from her errand.

Edwina was in her room, probably napping. Dirk had some paperwork he'd brought from the office, so I went to my room to freshen up and change. When I came down an hour later, dressed as I had been that morning, Dirk was in the salon at the table, going over some papers. Edwina was in her chair, reading.

"There you are, Allison," the old lady said cheerfully. "We were about to have our tea. Care to join us?"

"Yes, thank you." It was clear to me Mrs. Valescu hadn't said anything to Edwina. Not yet, anyway.

"Did you enjoy our little beach?"

"Very nice," I said, with a glance at Dirk. He had the look of the cat who'd eaten the canary. I could have smacked him, but he knew he was safe.

Edwina chatted away, saying that she'd had a very productive meeting with the attorney. She said they wanted to place David's affairs in my hands, with the condition I wouldn't attempt to have the court make a determination on his status. I took that to mean that she wanted me to formally acknowledge that David was alive until proven dead, which could be never.

I glanced at Dirk, who remained silent. I realized he could give me no help. "I suppose there's no harm in that for the time being," I said to Edwina.

When Mrs. Valescu brought the tea, I sat, quietly terrified. She scarcely looked my way, which came as a relief, and a bit of a surprise. I wondered if Dirk hadn't been right about her. After all, he'd known her a lot longer than I had.

When we'd finished tea, Dirk returned to his work and Edwina and I talked about inconsequential things. I was never much of a conversationalist, and I found this especially difficult. I not only felt like a criminal, but I was already looking ahead to the evening, and the next round of crime.

Dirk let me struggle with Edwina for half an hour before suggesting that we get ready for our evening out. He offered again to take Edwina, but she graciously refused.

"Show Allison the village. I want her to love this place as much as we do."

"I'll do my best, Aunt Edwina."

We got up to go to our rooms. Edwina stopped us. "I nearly forgot," she said. "This afternoon the sheriff's office called. They wanted us to know they watched the road off and on last night and they didn't see a trace of that man." She beamed. "Hopefully he went back to San Francisco, or wherever he was from."

"Let's hope so," Dirk said, giving me a long look.

Edwina sent us on our way with her blessing. Mrs. Valescu was waiting for us in the entry hall. She approached Dirk with scarcely a glance at me.

"Mr. Granville," she said in a low, discreet tone, "madam has instructed me to leave tonight after I've served her dinner. I understand you're going out for the evening. Do you want me to remain with her until your return, or shall I leave as instructed?"

"I think you should do as my aunt wishes," he replied.

"I do hate for her to be alone," the housekeeper said warily.

"That's between you and her. Mrs. Higson is quite capable of making decisions."

"Yes, sir. It's just that if you intend to be late, I thought I would insist on staying."

"I can't tell you when we'll return, Elena. I suggest you discuss my aunt's requirements with her."

Mrs. Valescu gave me a sly, disapproving look, the first of what I assumed would be many. "Yes, sir. I will."

We went upstairs.

"What do you suppose that was all about?" I asked as we stood in the hallway.

"I don't know. Maybe Mrs. Valescu is interested in some overtime."

"She's up to something, Dirk."

"What?"

"I don't know."

"Then there's no point in worrying about it."

"But I do worry. I don't like that woman. And by the looks of things, she doesn't like you much either, my dear. Maybe we shouldn't go to your house this evening," I whispered.

"To the contrary, all the more reason to go." He caressed my face. "Or would you prefer I make a midnight visit to your room?"

"Shh!"

Dirk chuckled.

"It's not funny. I've decided we won't do it again in this house."

"Then maybe you'll have to spend the rest of your visit at my place."

I gave him a meaningful look. "How do I dress tonight?"

"In something sexy."

"I don't have those sorts of clothes."

He leaned over and kissed me on the cheek. "Well, do the best you can. Maybe someday we can go shopping together."

"Are you an expert on women's clothes?" I teased.

"Well, I know what I like."

I'd never had a man go shopping with me. David and I had gone to Union Square together once before Christmas, but all we did was buy a present for Gloria. "Maybe sometime," I told Dirk.

He winked and went down the hall toward his room.

Despite the difficulties of the past few days, I was as close to being euphoric as I ever had been. I dared again to wonder if what I felt for Dirk Granville could be love. True, we hadn't known each other long, but just being around him made me feel so alive—like a young girl. David had never made me feel that way.

I understood now what Gloria was talking about when she had tried to describe passionate, heart-stopping love. A part of me wanted to rush to the phone and tell her that I had found it! With Dirk!

I looked through the clothes I'd brought, trying to decide what was sexiest. Not much was promising. I'd bought a forest-green knit suit when David and I were first dating. He'd never commented on it particularly, but I thought I was pretty in it, and the color was certainly nice with my hair. The suit wasn't sexy, but by rolling the waistband up a turn, I could shorten the skirt considerably. It was the best I could do, so I gave it a try.

I hadn't yet worn my hair up for Dirk and decided I would do that, too. Gloria had put it up for me once, saying I had a nice long neck and pretty ears, so I should show them off more. Necks were sexy, she'd said. But "sexy" had never been important to me until now.

Half an hour later Dirk knocked on my door. He was in a navy blazer, white cashmere turtleneck and steel-gray trousers. I looked at him and sighed. He seemed to approve of the way I looked, too, taking in my legs and short skirt with a sweep of his eye.

"You look beautiful, Allison." He took me in his arms and held me.

I put my head on his shoulder, inhaled his cologne and sighed again. "You know, whenever I stop to think about it, I realize how crazy this is."

"Life is crazy. Let's get out of this house."

Edwina was having her dinner when we went down. We said goodbye to her and, as she looked at us standing side by side in the doorway, an odd look passed over her face, replacing her smile.

I think she saw us as a couple, or maybe there was a telltale glow on my face that another man might not notice, but a woman would. Regardless, there was a tightness about her mouth as she urged us to have a good time.

We went out, getting into the Jaguar as darkness was falling. "She knows," I said, as we started down the drive.

"Aunt Edwina? You think so?"

"Yes. At least she's beginning to be suspicious."

"Well, if she is, she is. It can't be helped."

"Of course it can be helped. We can stop."

"Allison, we've hardly begun. Anyway, I don't care what she thinks. I don't want to hurt her unnecessarily, but we don't have to live our lives to suit her sensitivities."

"I can't afford to make an enemy of her," I said.

"Why not?"

It was a question for which I didn't have a precise answer. "No one needs enemies."

"As soon as David's situation is cleared up, you're going to end up with everything—even Edwina's share of Granville Lumber, once she's gone. I've talked to the lawyer, too. I already know that David's interest in the trust goes to you—as soon as he's legally declared dead, that is. Why do you think Edwina's trying to butter you up? Because she wants to keep things as they are now as long as she can."

"She also thinks David is alive. I know she does."

"I'm sure she's sincere about that. But the point is, you're the heir to half the company and Edwina can't do a thing about it."

I don't know whether I detected glee in Dirk's voice, or if it was only my imagination. I was in a stronger legal position than I had imagined. No wonder he was so unconcerned about our relationship being discovered.

Then an awful thought struck me. Had Dirk let the fact that I would become his partner upon Edwina's death influence his behavior toward me now? To put it more bluntly, did he care for me, or my interest in Granville Lumber?

And of course, there was that two million dollars floating around somewhere. He could be as interested in that as everyone else seemed to be.

I looked at him as we slowly made our way along the narrow road in the fading light. Dirk was as devastatingly handsome and sexy as ever, but suddenly there was doubt in my heart. I hated the feeling. Had I deceived myself? Even worse, had Dirk deceived me?

He moved on to discuss our plans for dinner. "We could go to the Eureka Inn," he said. "It's the most elegant place around, the closest we have to San Francisco dining."

"Whatever you want is fine, Dirk."

He reached over and took my hand. "When you're out with a beautiful woman, you want to show her off," he said, smiling.

I smiled back, but my heart wasn't in it. Euphoria one minute and despair the next. But was it justified? Or was it just paranoia on my part? After all, I hadn't ferreted out some dark secret. Dirk had come right out with the information himself. He wouldn't have willingly given me cause to doubt him, if it was true, would he?

My spirits rallied and I believed in him again. Then my self-doubt set in. No, I said to myself. He couldn't possibly love me. Only six months ago I was so socially inept I was afraid to shake a man's hand, let alone imagine myself becoming the love object of the most handsome man I'd ever laid eyes on. Dirk couldn't really care for me. He was using me. I was almost certain of it.

"I like your hair up, by the way," he said. "You have a nice neck. It's good to show it off."

I grimaced at the hypocrisy. What a phony! On the other hand, Gloria had said the same thing. Was it possible Dirk was sincere? I looked over at him, almost glaring. I wanted to grab him by the neck and demand the truth. Instead, I decided to lay low and play it cautious. "Thank you," I said sweetly.

The drive wasn't as pleasant as it could have been, considering my agony. Why couldn't he have kept his mouth shut and left me in ignorance?

We drove for a while in silence, skirting Arcata Bay. It was almost completely dark, but there was enough light to see the fog bank was lying off the coast. I shivered, deciding I hated this place and ought to get away from it. There was no reason to put myself through any more agony. I had the BMW; I could leave anytime I wished.

Yes, I would go back to San Francisco in the morning and let them fight it out any way they wished. After dinner, I would tell Dirk I didn't feel well. I'd ask him to take me home. And I'd keep my bedroom door locked.

"Everything all right, Allison?"

I looked over at him, surprised by the question. "Yes, why?"

"I don't know. You seem subdued."

I did my best to smile. "No, I'm just looking forward to a wonderful evening."

He took my hand again, rubbing the back of it with his thumb. "My, your hand's so cold."

"Cold hand, warm heart," I said.

Dirk grinned wryly, handsomely. It made me ache to look at him. Knowing he couldn't be trusted. But where, exactly did that leave me. I didn't know and I wasn't really sure I wanted to find out.

14

THE EUREKA INN was not what I expected. When Dirk pulled up under the porte cochere of the old English Tudor structure, I was amazed to discover that the hotel had an old-world atmosphere. That was even more true of the interior, with its polished brass, hardwoods and oil paintings.

Not having eaten at many of the finer places in San Francisco, I was excited at the prospect of elegant dining in the Rib Room. I even managed to put my annoyance with Dirk aside, taking his arm as we were escorted to our table. But once we were face-to-face in the tufted red leather booth, I started having trouble maintaining the pretense.

We'd only been seated a few moments when an elderly man, apparently a business acquaintance of Dirk's, came over to say hello. After we were introduced I tuned their conversation out, though I watched Dirk secretly, trying to assess whether or not my fears and suspicions about him were unfounded.

"It was a pleasure meeting you, Mrs. Higson," the elderly man said as he prepared to take his leave. "Sorry for the interruption."

Dirk had no sooner turned his attention back to me when another couple paused to say hello. The woman looked me over, but they didn't linger long enough for an introduction.

"You seem to be quite the big shot," I said after they'd gone.

"Is that sarcasm I detect?" he asked.

"Maybe."

"Allison, what's bothering you? Have I said something that offended you?"

"No."

"You just get moody for no reason every once in a while?"

"Yes, I suppose I do."

He didn't look pleased.

"Better you find out my flaws now rather than later," I said.

The waiter came to take drink orders, and Dirk asked if I wanted a cocktail or if I preferred wine. I told him to decide. He sent the waiter away.

"You aren't being straight with me," he said, when we were alone.

"Are you being straight with me, Dirk?"

"Meaning?"

"Just what I said."

"I'm a little dense, I'm afraid. Would you explain?"

"No, it isn't important."

"I think it's very important," he returned.

"Let's just try to enjoy dinner, okay? Then you can take me back."

"Back where?"

I flushed, realizing I'd jumped the gun. I was supposed to wait until after dinner to tell him I wasn't feeling well, but I'd spoken without thinking. "Never mind."

"You're upset about Aunt Edwina being suspicious about us."

"No. Well, yes. I mean, maybe." I picked up my water glass and took a long drink, only to find Dirk chuckling. "It's not funny," I said.

"Allison, will you quit this nonsense and tell me what's wrong."

I stared at him hard and long, expecting his face to dissolve in guilt. It didn't. He returned my gaze fearlessly. Eventually I gave in and looked away.

"Please, Allison," he said, not quite but almost begging, "talk to me."

"The truth is you don't give a damn about me," I blurted out. "Not really. You're wooing me because when Edwina dies I'm going to control the other half of Granville Lumber. And in the meantime I've got two million dollars that could come in handy. That's what this is really about, isn't it, Dirk?"

"You aren't kidding, are you?"

"No, I'm not kidding."

"For a second, there, I thought you were summarizing the plot of a soap opera."

"Don't be sarcastic."

"Well, could you explain where you got this notion?" he demanded.

"It just came to me. I was trying to figure out why you were courting me, then I saw the whole thing."

He smirked. "Did it ever occur to you that you might be wrong? That maybe I do happen to care for you?"

His words were smooth as silk. I looked for the hole in them, sure it couldn't be explained away that easily. The waiter returned and Dirk, unwilling to let me off the hook, sent the man away a second time.

"So?" he said.

"Well, what's wrong with my argument?"

"You're presupposing quite a bit. Say we become lovers—long-term, even. That doesn't get me your share of Granville Lumber, does it?"

"It's a start."

"We'd have to marry, Allison. Even then, I wouldn't have it unless you gave it to me. It would be your separate property."

"Edwina's husband ran the company for her, didn't he?"

"I already run the company."

I was beginning to see my theory was not without holes. But I wasn't yet ready to give up. I toyed with my fork, thinking.

"Look," Dirk said, "I haven't asked you to marry me yet, so until I do, give me the benefit of the doubt, okay? There's also another small problem."

"What's that?"

"You're married."

"Officially, maybe."

Dirk smiled. "That's probably good enough to keep us from the altar. For the time being, anyway."

"You're making fun of me," I snapped.

"You're the one who made the accusations. I was minding my own business, thinking I was taking a lovely woman out to dinner—someone I happen to be very attracted to. But you've turned it into a shooting match. Maybe you owe me an apology."

I wasn't through. "What about the money?"

"What about it?"

"Maybe that's what you're after."

"I suppose that's possible." He sighed.

"Well?"

"Well, before you prepare to hang me, maybe you should wait and see if I ask you where the money is. If I don't ask, it could be because I don't care about it, because I'm innocent. I know that messes up your theory, but you would rather me be a good guy than a bad guy, wouldn't you?"

I could see I'd been had. "You're really enjoying this, aren't you, Dirk?"

"No relationship is perfect," he replied. "If we didn't have at least one little spat, I would have begun doubting things myself."

"All right," I told him, "I jumped to conclusions. But you can certainly see why."

Dirk reached over and took my hand. "Allison," he said, "for a long time now I've had everything I could possibly want in life, with one exception. And it's possible, just possible, you may be the solution to that. I don't mean to scare you by making such an ominous statement, but it happens to be true."

I held Dirk's hand in both of mine. "You're very clever, aren't you?" I said.

"What do you mean by that?"

"You've set this up so that you can't lose."

The corners of his mouth twitched. "You wouldn't hold that against me, would you?"

With a silent nod to my friend Gloria, I said, "I'm a sincere person, Dirk, but I'm not above using you every bit as much as you're willing to use me. So be on your guard."

He laughed and beckoned the waiter to come take our orders.

I DIDN'T KNOW IF I WAS a fool for suspecting Dirk in the first place, or for granting him his innocence now. But being friends was certainly more enjoyable than being enemies. As we progressed through dinner I again let my hopes resurface.

I hardly noticed what I ate. Dirk had a way, I discovered, of seducing without touching. Little comments he made, looks he gave, aroused me, made me want to be alone with him. I couldn't wait until we'd had our coffee and were on our way.

As we waited at the hotel entrance for the car to be brought around, Dirk was greeted by another man, coming in the door. They chatted for several minutes and the man, a heavyset fellow, was introduced to me as Ed Carlson, a shift boss at the mill.

"Oh, one thing I wanted to mention, Dirk," Carlson said. "Charlie Smith came by this afternoon, drunk as usual. But he had a funny story that didn't seem to be just booze talkin'. Said there's a squatter that's been livin' up at your cabin the past couple of weeks. He told me about it, then asked for a ten-spot. It could have been just somethin' he made up for whiskey money, but I thought you ought to know about it."

Dirk thought for a moment. "Hmm. Thanks, Ed, for letting me know."

"I can have one of the crews swing by when one's headed that way, if you want, Dirk."

"No, that's all right. I might drive up and have a look myself. The place hasn't been checked out since fall, so it's time I go up anyway. But I appreciate the offer."

"Oh, there's one other thing. Charlie said somebody's been visiting this guy. Drives up a couple of times a week."

"Any idea who the visitor is?"

Carlson shook his head. "Charlie didn't say. Don't think he knew."

Dirk nodded. The man saluted him and went on inside the hotel.

I looked at Dirk and he looked at me. I saw something in his eyes.

"Who's Charlie Smith?" I asked.

"An old man who worked at the mill for many years. He had a drinking problem and finally went on disability. He lives back in the woods. Never was sharp, and the booze finally cooked his brain. He's always full of fantastic tales."

The car arrived and we got in. Moments later we were on our way back to Arcata.

"You have a cabin?" I asked.

"It's a family place, actually. Belongs to all of us. I spent a lot of weekends and holidays there as a kid."

"Presumably David did, as well."

"Yes," Dirk replied, "David, too."

I didn't say what I was thinking, and Dirk didn't comment further, though we had to be wondering the same thing. But I'd already done a lot of accusing and speculating that evening and I didn't see anything to be gained by opening another can of worms.

Dirk took my hand and kissed it. "Ever been to a man's place to see his etchings before?" he asked.

I chuckled. "Of course not. We decided I was almost a virgin bride, remember?"

"Yes, we did decide that," he teased. "But I'm not so sure I believe it anymore. You might secretly be one of the world's great lovers."

"Now, isn't that a case of the pot calling the kettle black?"

He rubbed my knuckles against his cheek. "This has been a very slow evening, Allison."

"Why? Because the company's been dull?"

He kissed my hand once more. "No, because I've been waiting for dessert."

I smiled in the darkness of the car. I didn't care again. About anything.

DIRK'S PLACE WAS IN THE mountains above the town of Arcata. The slopes were covered with redwoods and we were soon driving on a narrow twisty road through the forest. In the darkness the trees were like sleeping giants, standing broad-shouldered along the sides of the road, their tops extending out of sight into the night sky.

I watched the headlights of the car sweep back and forth across the road in front of us. We passed an occasional driveway and mailbox, but the isolation was evident, even though we were only a few minutes from town.

We were going around a sharp curve when all of a sudden headlights flashed into our vision. An oncoming car appeared from nowhere, nearly colliding with us. Dirk slammed on the brakes and swerved to the edge of the road. We came to a dead stop. The engine had died, but a sound was still ringing in my ears. I think it was a yelp I'd let out when I thought we were about to crash.

"That was close," Dirk said. "I wonder who that maniac was. I don't think it was one of my neighbors. The car didn't look familiar." He glanced over at me.

I was staring straight ahead. My heart was tripping. But it wasn't just from the near collision.

"You all right, Allison?"

"Did you see the color of that car?" I asked.

"No, frankly I didn't notice."

"It was brown."

He stared at me. "You think it was your buddy?"

"I didn't get a very good look. But it could have been."

Dirk didn't say a word. He started the car, put it in gear and hurried on up the road. In another minute we were at Dirk's place, a modern home built on the side of the mountain amid the redwoods. There was hardly time to admire it, though. It was brightly lit by floodlights and a burglar alarm was blaring.

Dirk jumped out, cautioning me to wait in the car. He disappeared inside. In a moment the alarm was off and the lights dimmed except for a warmly glowing porch light. One moment the place looked like a prison under siege; the next, like a tranquil and inviting retreat.

Dirk came back to the car and opened my door. "I think you were right, Allison," he said. "That was probably your friend we almost ran into."

"Did he break in?"

"He tried to. The alarm went off and he probably panicked. It's hooked up to the police, so he was smart to hightail it out of here." Dirk offered me his hand and helped me out of the car.

"Are the police coming?"

"No, I called them and said not to bother."

"Don't you want them to investigate?"

He put an arm around my shoulders as we walked toward the front door. "I've got more important things to do this evening. Besides, the guy never made it inside. No harm done. Just a broken window."

We went into the house. It was all wood and glass, completely modern and with multilevels. There were lots of big leafy plants. The furnishings were bold, comfortable, masculine. The art and decor were Native American—contemporary and tasteful. The house was spacious, but not large. It looked like Dirk.

One side of the structure was almost completely glass. Dirk assured me that by day the broad expanse of the Pacific was visible, but all I could see then was darkness and a few stars twinkling high overhead. We were above the fog that had moved in.

We stood there at the window for a time, then Dirk kissed me. "You wouldn't have staged a burglary just to throw me off track, would you?" I asked, pressing my face into his neck.

"You may never know," he said, chuckling.

Dirk got us each a glass of sherry and showed me the master suite. It was half a level higher and, like the great room, it had a view of the unseen ocean. There was a deck off it with a spa. We stepped out and I hugged myself against the chill of the night air. While I stood at the railing, sipping my sherry, Dirk pushed a button and the water in the spa began bubbling.

"That," he said, pointing at the steamy water, "is the most relaxing place on earth after a rough day."

I wondered if the day I'd had would qualify.

Dirk apparently read my thoughts, because he put his arm around me and said, "Care for a dip to relax a little?"

"I don't suppose suits are required?"

He kissed my hair. "Not for world-class lovers."

I had to laugh at his words. Allison Stephens a world-class lover! If my friends back in San Francisco could hear Dirk say that, they would laugh, too. Maybe I was the one putting on an act, not Dirk.

I used the bathroom to undress and when I came out onto the deck, a large bath towel wrapped around me, he was already in the water. I stood there for a moment, staring at him. "Did you cheat and put on a suit?" I asked.

"No. Want me to stand up to prove it?"

"That's all right. I trust you." I went to the edge of the spa, descended knee-deep to the first step, unwrapped the towel and tossed it aside, then eased into the steaming water and Dirk Granville's embrace.

The sensation of the hot water on my clammy flesh was exquisite, but the sensation of Dirk's arms was even better. We kissed and caressed each other.

"Good, Lord," I said between kisses, "do you do this often? If I lived here, I'd spend my life in the spa."

"It's not the same alone."

I pushed him an arm's length away. "Dirk, I'll never, as long as I live, believe you have trouble finding women to share this with."

He pulled me to him and kissed me on the mouth. "Finding women isn't the issue," he muttered. "It's caring about them."

Dirk pulled me onto his lap and I straddled him. He caressed my breasts, making them tingle. The longer he did it, the farther the charge spread though my body until even my toes were alive with sensation. I reached down and found his penis, taking it in both my hands.

Dirk lay back against the edge of the spa, closing his eyes as I stroked him. He was long and hard and I wanted to put him inside me so we could float weightlessly, our bodies coupled.

Dirk smiled. "I thought you were supposed to be a shy little thing."

"Maybe," I said coyly, "when a woman loses her emotional virginity, she loses her inhibitions, too."

Dirk curled his finger, signaling me to come to him. Slowly I floated closer, parting my legs when I got to him, and wrapping them around his waist.

He was still hard as steel but he slipped right into me. The sensation was unique. There was no weight, no pressure, only Dirk's considerable manhood filling me.

I had hold of his shoulders and he had my hips, gyrating me against him. I could feel him in me, but all other contact was feathery light. Every nerve in my body was focused on the point of penetration. I purred and moaned and writhed, unable to get enough of him.

When Dirk took a firm hold of my hips and arched, his final thrust nearly lifted me from the water. I felt him gush and then I climaxed, wave after wave rippling through me until I collapsed on him, exhausted.

Dirk, breathing as heavily as I, held on to me. Our faces and hair were soaked with steam. We kissed languorously.

Dirk looked at me through hooded eyes. He was spent. "God," he said.

I pressed my cheek against his. "Yes," I whispered into his ear. "I agree."

When we found the strength, we climbed out of the spa, dried ourselves and staggered to the bed. I knew at some point we had to go back to Edwina's, but at that moment I didn't care if it took a hundred years.

Dirk held me, as we lay with the covers draped over our bodies. I snuggled as close to him as I could, knowing that in moments I would be asleep.

Sometime later I awoke to the touch of his hand between my legs. He'd aroused me even before I was fully awake.

We made love twice more, the first time with him behind me on his knees, lifting my buttocks as he drove himself exquisitely into my body. The second time we lay side by side and he kissed me tenderly—my face, my neck, my shoulders and arms. It was as gentle as any lovemaking I'd ever known. My orgasm that time seemed to go on endlessly.

After that last time we lay in each other's arms, staring at the arched ceiling. Dirk was stroking my cheek.

"David's alive, isn't he?" I said, finally saying out loud the unspoken thought that had made our lovemaking so frenzied, so . . . final. "He's the one who that Charlie person saw at the cabin."

There was a long silence. Then he murmured, "I don't know. I guess we'll find out tomorrow."

15

SUNRISE WAS ONLY A FEW hours away by the time we finally made it back to Edwina's. I felt contrite having left the poor woman alone for all those hours, but it bothered me a lot more to think that David might be really alive and living in a cabin not too many miles away. Dirk and I said good-night in the hallway, then went to our rooms.

Alone in my bed, I was tormented by my gut instinct that told me that my husband was indeed very much alive.

I managed to get some sleep, but was awake by seven. The house seemed quiet. I showered and dressed and went downstairs to find Edwina being served breakfast. My mother-in-law stared at me with an icy gaze. She knew.

"Good morning," I said, taking my seat. "Isn't Dirk up yet?"

"I don't know how *you* managed to get up," Edwina snapped, "considering it was after four by the time you and Dirk got home."

I lowered my eyes, suddenly incapable of lying. "I'm very sorry," I said. "I was afraid we'd disturb you."

"What if something had happened to madam!" Mrs. Valescu interjected. "A fire. Illness. Anything."

"That's enough, Elena!" David's mother said. "It's not your affair. Please, just go and prepare Allison's breakfast." When the housekeeper had left, Edwina said, "I won't ask what you were doing. I prefer to believe you're a moral woman. But I certainly won't be a party to questionable behavior. I'm asking Dirk to leave here at once. I don't think it appropriate that you see him anymore."

I sighed, hating the fact that I was being chastised, but knowing I deserved it. And I couldn't even defend myself by declaring that my husband was dead.

"Did I hear my name mentioned?" It was Dirk at the doorway, looking chipper and energetic. He was in jeans and a deep blue sweater, his hair still wet from his shower.

"Dirk," Edwina said, "I should like to speak with you later."

"Certainly," he replied, taking his place at the table. "But I want to apologize first for coming in so late. I hope we didn't disturb you. By the time we finished with the police it was practically dawn."

"Police? What are you talking about?"

"Didn't Allison tell you? My house was burglarized last evening. One of the sheriff's deputies saw us leaving the Eureka Inn and flagged me down. We think it was the same guy who's been tormenting Allison."

Edwina looked at me with shock. "Why didn't you tell me, dear? Here I was accusing you. I'm so sorry."

I turned to her and shrugged. "I didn't want to upset you." Dirk had a little smile on his face and I didn't know whether to be grateful or ashamed of our lie. In the end, I rationalized that it did Edwina no good to know the truth. Better she live with her delusions.

"What did you mean by the word *accusing*, Aunt Edwina?" Dirk asked with mock innocence.

"It was nothing," I interjected. "We were having a little disagreement about David. It was a misunderstanding. Nothing important."

The old woman smiled appreciatively. "You're quite a young woman, Allison," she said. "David is very fortunate to have you. And I was completely mistaken about you. Dirk, I'm ashamed to say I've wrongfully accused you both, and I apologize for that."

"Well," Dirk said cheerfully, "I am guilty of monopolizing her time. And I plan to keep her busy today. I want to show her the mill and some of our timber properties, maybe take her by the cabin up at the lake. We'll be leaving right after breakfast, but with luck, I'll have her back in time for tea."

Edwina nodded her approval. I felt sick at being such a fraud. But Dirk and I had very serious work to do—work we couldn't share with Edwina. That helped me to rationalize, though I still felt very badly.

I happened to glance up as Edwina asked Dirk about the burglary and saw the kitchen door soundlessly ease shut. Mrs. Valescu had been listening again.

FORTY-FIVE MINUTES later Dirk and I were on the freeway, headed north. "Your aunt had us figured out," I told him, "until you cleverly diverted her with that story."

"I know. I was listening in the hall."

"Are you always so nimble?" I asked.

"What do you mean?"

"It's hard to know when you're telling the truth and when you're not. You're a consummate actor."

He reached over and caressed my neck. "With you, Allison, I'm a hundred-percent honest. You can count on that."

"I want to . . . badly," I said. "Believe me, I do."

"I know. It will just take some time, I guess. But right now I'm more worried about what we're going to find at the cabin. Aunt Edwina's certainty about David still being alive is not looking as ridiculous as it did before I heard about the squatter."

"Well, if she's right, the future is going to be a lot more complicated," I said blackly.

"Yes, and I've been thinking about the burglary last night. This friend of yours who's been causing all the trouble is a very serious man."

"At least you can see why I've been so upset."

"I don't mean to add to your anxiety, Allison, but did you notice that Mrs. Valescu left the house right after she finished serving breakfast?"

"No, did she?"

"While you were upstairs."

"What does that mean?"

"I don't know, but things are getting more and more fishy."

We left the freeway and followed a narrow, paved road into the mountains. After a while we turned onto a gravel logging road that wound through the wooded slopes to the edge of a lake that shone blue in the sunlight. On the low ridge above it the road branched into several different tracks. Dirk stopped the car.

"Charlie Smith lives up at that end of the lake, back in the woods. Our cabin's around this other way," he said, pointing.

My dread had been escalating, mile by mile. I didn't know if I could handle seeing David, though I knew my feelings for him were dead. I was almost afraid to find out the truth, yet I knew I had no choice.

Dirk drove very slowly because the road was rough. We were going through dense forest when he suddenly stopped.

"We're fairly close now. I think we should go in on foot," he said. "Or, if you prefer, you can wait here."

"No, I want to come."

"Don't slam the door shut. The sound might alert whoever is at the cabin."

We got out and began walking along the track. The woods seemed so still, the sound of birds singing so incongruous with the high drama that was unfolding. Dirk took my hand, which made me feel better. I couldn't believe my life had come to this—sneaking through the woods with my lover to try to discover if my dead husband was really alive.

Dirk stopped as a building came into view through the trees. "There's a car," he said.

We moved from tree to tree, getting as close as we could without being seen. Dirk peered around a large redwood and I leaned against it, my body wired, my nerves near breaking point. My heart was pounding.

"It's a brown sedan," he whispered.

Holding my breath, I peeked around the tree. Dirk was right. "You mean the guy who's been after me has been staying here? Not David?" I whispered.

"Maybe."

I wasn't sure whether to be glad or not. Things were much too confusing to be sure of anything now.

"I'd better have a look," Dirk said. "It's my place. I have a right to know who's in my cabin."

"No. You can't go. Not unarmed. That man's dangerous. He might hurt you."

"So far, he's only tormented people."

"You don't know that for sure," I said.

"I've got to find out what's going on, Allison. You stay here."

I wasn't eager to go, but I didn't want Dirk going, either. I took hold of him and pulled his face close to mine. "I love you," I whispered. "Please be careful."

Dirk smiled and kissed my lips. Then he crept around the tree and moved toward the cabin. I watched him for a while, but when he got to the window on the side of the cabin, I couldn't take it anymore. I leaned against the tree, my arms folded and clutched against my chest. A long minute of silence passed, then I heard Dirk's voice.

"Allison, you can come out. It's safe."

I peeked around the tree and saw Dirk on the small covered porch. He stepped down off it as I walked toward the cabin. He came partway to meet me. His expression was grim.

"David's not here," he said, knowing that would be my first question. "But your friend is. And he's dead."

THERE WAS NO TELEPHONE in the cabin and Dirk told me we would have to drive a few miles to get to the nearest one. He took me by the arm, but I didn't want to leave without having a look inside for myself.

"It's not pretty," he said. "The guy has a big hole in his chest and there's lots of blood. He's been shot."

"I have to see what he looks like."

Dirk stepped aside, and I went to the cabin. I climbed onto the porch, knowing the sight would be unpleasant. I had to know for sure that it wasn't David. That was being distrustful of Dirk, but I wanted reassurance, not only about him, but about the state of my life.

The dead man was a stranger. Staring at his face, I asked myself if he could be the one who'd broken into my apartment and made me fall down the stairs. I asked myself if he could have followed me in Golden Gate Park, on Ocean Beach. The brown sedan was parked outside. There was a good chance he'd at least been the man who'd followed me up the Redwood Highway from San Francisco.

I glanced around, looking for some evidence of David. I had no idea what had happened here, and at this point nobody could even say if the dead man had been the squatter; but considering all the trouble I'd been having in San Francisco, I didn't see how he could be both here and there at the same time.

There were two bedrooms. One appeared untouched, the other was obviously well used. There were clothes and other personal effects. I looked them over without touching anything but could find nothing that I knew to be my husband's. Was it possible David had died in the murky waters of the bay, after all?

I turned to leave and found Dirk standing in the doorway. "What are you doing?" he asked gently.

"I . . ." Suddenly I was overwhelmed by emotion. My face crumpled and I began to cry. Dirk folded me into his arms. I sniffled, regaining control. "I was wondering if David might have been here," I explained.

"Do you think he was?"

"I don't know," I said. "But somebody killed this man."

AFTER PHONING THE SHERIFF, we waited for the authorities at the head of the logging road, then returned with them to the cabin. The deputies talked to us until the lab unit arrived. About then, Dirk asked if we could leave, saying they could contact us at his place.

We drove to Arcata in silence. I was emotionally spent. It was past lunchtime when we got there and Dirk offered to fix me something, but I wasn't hungry.

"Do you suppose we should tell Edwina?" I asked, as I curled up in a big chair that afforded a misty view of the Pacific.

"She'll find out soon enough," he replied. "I don't see any point in rushing to give her the grim news."

"We've spared her everything else," I said sardonically. "I suppose we can spare her this, too."

Dirk and I spent a doleful afternoon. For a while he sat with me, holding my hand. We went out onto the deck and got a brace of ocean air as we stared at the view. Far out to sea, dark ominous clouds were piling up on the horizon. A storm was on the way.

We talked a little about what had happened, knowing that the murder had made the entire situation much graver than it had been before. When I'd come to Arcata I'd been anxious and troubled; the murder and the possibility that David was alive had pushed things to the brink of terror.

"You know, the police in the Bay Area were questioning whether the death of David's partner was really accidental," I said to Dirk. "I wonder if that could have been a murder, too. And if so, if they are somehow connected."

"There's only one common link that I can see," Dirk replied.

He didn't have to explain—the common link was David.

We decided that the man who'd been harassing me, the dead man, wouldn't have been at the family cabin due to some sort of coincidence. That, too, had to be connected with David. But why would David have wanted him there, assuming that David was alive?

Late in the afternoon Dirk got a call from the sheriff's office. He was on the phone for a long time before coming back to tell me what he'd learned.

"They've identified the dead man. His name is Jack Bates. He's an ex-con from San Francisco with a long criminal record. Fraud, extortion, grand theft, assault and a host of smaller crimes."

"Good Lord, this was the man who was following me?"

Dirk sat on the sofa next to me. "The sheriff has been talking to the San Francisco police and they're trying to make a connection. They don't believe Bates was staying at the cabin. They feel he was a visitor and that whoever has been living there could be the killer."

"How do they know that?"

"Bates is a big man. The clothing they found was too small for him. They're doing lab work on the personal effects and hope to come up with something. I asked them to keep me informed."

Dirk persuaded me that we should go out for some dinner. He wanted to get my mind off what had happened. I told him I would go, but that I felt we ought to at least call Edwina to let her know we'd been delayed.

"What shall I tell her we're doing?" he asked.

"You seem to be pretty good at coming up with stories," I chided. "Use your imagination."

Dirk gave me a look and went off to telephone. When he came back he seemed nonplussed.

"What's wrong?" I asked. "Couldn't you come up with a story she'd buy?"

"No, that's not it. Aunt Edwina is in good spirits and she was appreciative of the call. We're still virtuous in her eyes."

"Then why are you looking so strange?"

"She told me Elena Valescu has been gone all day, that she never returned from her errand. Aunt Edwina hasn't been able to track her down."

"Your poor aunt. Is she frightened?"

"No, she's as independent as any woman's ever been. It's always others who are concerned. But she is worried about Mrs. Valescu. I told her we'd come as soon as we can, probably after we eat."

"What will Edwina do for dinner?" I asked, genuinely concerned.

"She can get around the kitchen. She told me she'd be fine."

Dirk drove me in to Arcata and we decided to spend a little time looking around before choosing a restaurant. It was a nice change to be out among people. We browsed in bookstores and shops, finally ending up at a vegetarian café a block or so away from the main square.

The place was relatively quiet and we sat at a table in the back. After we ordered, Dirk took my hands, holding them as we gazed into each other's eyes.

"I know this has been a rough day," he said.

"I'm glad we were together, Dirk. I don't know how I'd have gotten through these last few days without you."

He looked at me with those compelling dark eyes that in the course of only a few days had become more loving than mysterious. "Allison," he said, his voice trembling with emotion, "however this turns out, whether David is alive or dead, I want you to know that I love you."

My eyes filled and I pulled his hands to my mouth so that I could kiss them. "Oh, Dirk," I murmured. "That means so much to me. I can't tell you."

He rubbed my fingers anxiously, but with affection. "It was hard at first, finding myself falling in love with you, knowing you'd married David. And yet I believe so strongly that we belong together."

I understood his anxiety, for I'd suffered in the same way. In the midst of my greatest sorrow, Dirk had come into my life. At first he'd been my tormentor, obsessing me day and night. Now he was my lover, the man I cared for deeply. And miraculously, wonderfully, Dirk cared for me, too. But there had been a sword over our heads from the start, and the sword was David.

We left the restaurant as darkness was falling. The wind had come up, blowing dark clouds in from the ocean, the leading edge of a big storm. Raindrops began spattering the pavement as we got to the car.

"Shall we go back to my place?" Dirk asked.

"I think we should go to Edwina's. She's been alone all day." Judging by his expression I could tell Dirk was not pleased with the idea, but he relented.

As we drove north toward Trinidad, the wind began blowing even harder and the rain pelted the windshield. It was dreary and cold and were it not for Dirk, I could have fallen into a dark mood. So many terrible things had happened, and I didn't understand what was behind them.

I looked at Dirk, his face illuminated by the headlights of the oncoming cars. He seemed strong and resolute as ever, but I could tell he was troubled, too.

"What's going to happen?" I whispered. "What will become of us?"

"It will settle eventually. Then you and I are going away together. Hawaii, Tahiti, it doesn't matter. Someplace warm and sunny."

I put my head on his shoulder. "I can't tell you how marvelous that sounds."

"Maybe I'll call my travel agent tomorrow," he said. "What the hell, we don't need to stick around here. We can leave right away."

"I'd rather know everything was resolved, that we wouldn't be coming back to more of the same thing."

He caressed my face. "Maybe you're right."

We fell silent, each retreating into our thoughts, watching the storm that was now attacking with a vengeance.

The road to Edwina's was slippery. The pavement was narrow to begin with, but the reduced visibility made the cliff doubly terrifying. It was like driving along the edge of an abyss. I stared past the wipers that swished back and forth across the glass, my hands gripping the seat.

We had passed the most hazardous part when Dirk said, "Allison, I don't feel right sitting around. I've got to do what I can to get to the bottom of this mess."

"But what can you do? The police are investigating the murder."

"I know, but I've been thinking about Mrs. Valescu. It's not like her to disappear. She's generally conscientious. But she was also very fond of David. I'm suspicious that she knows more than she's letting on."

"Like what?"

"I have no idea. But I want to talk to her. If you don't mind, I'll drop you off and see if I can find her. She has a house on the other side of Trinidad."

"Why don't you let the police handle it?"

"What can I tell them? That she's a suspicious old lady who was devoted to my dead cousin?"

Finally the house came into view. I had wanted to return out of a sense of obligation, but seeing the old Victorian, especially after Dirk had said he wanted to go out again, made me regret my decision. To bolster my resolve I tried to think of poor Edwina, confined to her wheelchair, having spent the day alone.

Dirk parked the car and turned off the engine. With the rain pounding against the windshield, the gale seemed even more threatening than before.

"I wish you would stay," I said.

"I won't be long. Mrs. Valescu may not even be home. I just have to do something."

I must have looked very unhappy because Dirk took my face in his hands. I could sense his smile in the darkness.

"I'll walk you to the door and let you in with my key so that Aunt Edwina doesn't have to," he said.

"There's no reason for us both to get soaked," I protested.

Dirk reached into the back seat for his trench coat. "In this part of the country one must always be prepared during the rainy season. I'll come get you."

He jumped out of the car and came around to my side. Holding the coat over our heads, we ran up the steps. The outside light wasn't on, though a soft glow came from the curtained windows on either side of the door. Because of the wind, we'd gotten fairly wet despite the coat.

Dirk didn't open the door right away. He took me into his arms as we huddled together, protected from the wind and rain. I looked up at him, seeing his skin glistening with raindrops. He kissed me and I kissed him back, clinging to him as long as I could. Dirk whispered that he loved me and that he wouldn't be long.

"Drive safely," I said, and kissed him a last time.

Unlocking the door, he let me into the silent, dimly lit house. I immediately turned to the window and saw him descend the steps, his trench coat flying over him in the gale. Moments later I heard the car start. Then I watched him going down the drive until the taillights disappeared in the gloom.

I turned around, focusing my attention on the house. I listened, but could hear no sound except the faint ticking of the clock in the salon and the tattoo of the rain on the roof. I wondered if Edwina was in bed, whether I was too late to keep her company.

I moved to the entrance to the salon. It was lit by a softly glowing lamp. Edwina was in her chair at the bay window, staring out at the night. The pane was like a mirror. I could see her face in it, and she could see me.

Edwina slowly turned to face me. "Where's Dirk?" she asked somberly.

I was surprised by her tone, and also to see what looked like tears running down her cheeks. "Mrs. Higson, what's wrong?"

"Where's Dirk?" she repeated.

"He had something to do. He dropped me off, but he'll return later."

"That's good," she said, "because I would have had to send him away."

I edged closer to her. She was crying. "What's happened?" I asked. "Are you all right?"

"Never mind me, Allison. You must go to your room." Her voice trembled as she spoke.

A dark feeling came over me. "Why?"

Edwina's mouth opened, her lip trembled. "My son is there. He's waiting for you."

16

I TOOK A STEP BACK. A sudden chill went through me as I searched Edwina's eyes for an explanation, and I absently rubbed my arms. My mind was spinning as the horror—all the implications of her announcement—started sinking in.

"Don't be afraid, Allison," she said with a tremulous voice. "He's your husband."

"I...know," I murmured. "But...why did he... I don't understand what's happened."

"The important thing is that he's here for you. He came back for you, Allison. You must go to him."

I turned toward the doorway, hating the fact that Dirk wasn't with me, that I was alone. I considered running away, but what would I be escaping from? The truth?

"I told you he would come back," Edwina said softly. "There's no reason to be afraid."

But I was afraid. I was deathly afraid, though I didn't fear for my physical safety. It had never entered my mind that David could hurt me, because I was sure he wouldn't. But I was afraid for my emotional well-being. I was afraid for my future. My life, my hope, had suddenly been wrenched from me.

"Would you rather I call him down?" my mother-in-law asked.

"No," I said, backing away. "I'll go up."

I slowly walked from the salon to the hall, lingering at the foot of the stairs. My heart was raging. Even the storm seemed to pale beside the turmoil within me. I put my hand on the rail and took the first step, then the second. What would I say to him? What would he say to me?

David Higson was my husband, but I no longer knew him. I was no longer his wife—not in my heart of hearts. I resolved to tell him that. I would explain that he'd violated my trust, destroyed what love there was between us. My heart was free of him, even if I was not.

A soft light was coming from under the door to my bedroom. I didn't knock. I turned the knob and pushed the door open.

David was sitting in the chair by the bay window, facing me. He slowly rose to his feet, the man I'd married on that rainy day in December. He looked gaunt, his expression somber as he stared at me. He was in a white shirt and gray trousers. He had on a Windbreaker that was unzipped, and he looked as though he'd just come home, maybe from having been for a walk before the rain started.

I didn't move from the doorway. David didn't move, either. We stared at each other for a long minute.

"Can you forgive me, Allison?" he finally said.

"Why did you do it? How could you let me believe you were dead? How could you do that to me, David?"

He looked anguished, as though at any moment he might cry. "I had no choice," he murmured.

I closed the door, leaning against it because I barely had the strength to stand. I could no longer imagine myself loving this man. He took a couple of tentative steps in my direction. I tensed. He stopped.

"Allison," he said. "I love you."

I shook my head in disbelief.

"Yes, you must believe me. This has been hard for me, too—the most difficult experience of my life."

"Tell me about it. I still don't know what happened. One day the police come to me and say you've drowned. Now, a couple of months later, you show up alive. Don't you think I'm entitled to know what's going on?"

"I'll explain everything eventually. But right now we have to go. We have to get away from here. Tonight."

"I don't have to do anything."

David came closer, taking me by the arms. I recoiled, but he gave me a shake. "Don't fight me over this," he pleaded. He let go of me and turned to pace, pausing to glance back at me. He looked sullen, even angry. "What's going on between you and Dirk?"

"That's not the issue."

"It *is* the issue, Allison. You're my wife. I've come back at a great risk to myself. I'd hoped to come sooner, but he wouldn't give up. He wouldn't stop."

"*Who* wouldn't stop?"

David continued pacing, muttering to himself about getting on a plane to South America. It was then I realized he'd slipped over the edge. I'd been so preoccupied with trying to understand what was happening, that I didn't notice the fragile state he was in.

"Tell me, David," I said. "Tell me why you disappeared."

He looked confused. I took him by the arm and led him back to the chair where he'd been sitting. As I sat down at the foot of the bed, I noticed a sports bag on the floor beside his chair.

"I'm waiting," I said.

David sighed and rubbed his forehead for a moment before speaking. "It was the only way I could think of to get rid of him. I figured if he thought I was dead, he would give up. Even though I knew you were suffering, I couldn't come to you until it was safe. And I couldn't tell you, because that would have put you in even more danger. When you came up here to see my mother, I decided this was the time. But he followed you."

David had a crazed look in his eyes. I listened, unsure what to do.

"He didn't deserve any more money," David went on. "He was paid for what he'd done. But he wasn't satisfied. He wanted my money, too. He was blackmailing me. And I knew eventually he'd want it all."

"You're talking about the insurance money."

"Yes. It was mine. I put my trust in Robert and he failed me. I had no choice. I had to do it."

David started to cry. He leaned over and buried his face in his hands, sobbing for a minute. He finally stopped, looking up at me plaintively.

"You had Robert killed, didn't you? You had him run off the road while we were in Mexico on our honeymoon."

David nodded, tears streaming down his cheeks. "Don't you see, I was going to lose everything. The insurance money was my only hope."

"So you hired Jack Bates to kill Robert Willis."

He lowered his eyes. "Yes."

"And after you faked your death, Bates assumed I had the money. That's why he's been harassing me."

"I didn't know about that, Allison. I didn't find out until you got here."

"Who told you?"

"Elena. I was staying at our cabin. She brought me food and supplies. She promised to tell me when you came, so that we could go away together." He leaned over and picked up the sports bag. "Darling, I have two million dollars in bearer bonds here. We're set for life. In two days we can be in South America."

"I'm not going with you, David."

He looked stunned, disbelieving. "But why not? You love me, don't you? Nothing has changed."

"*Everything* has changed."

A dark look came over him. "It *is* Dirk. Elena told me, but I didn't believe her."

"Dirk isn't the reason. I wouldn't go with you even if I'd never met him. How could I, after what you've done?"

"This money is mine, Allison!" he shouted. "I deserve it!"

"You killed for it. Not only Robert Willis, but Jack Bates, too."

"Jack followed Elena to the cabin. He would have killed me if I hadn't gotten him first. It was self-defense."

"Robert wasn't self-defense." Tears filled my eyes.

David stood. He came to the bed, setting the bag beside me. "Allison, you don't understand. I did this for you, too. For us. I took a big chance coming here tonight. I love you. Don't you understand that?"

I regarded him through the blur of my tears. "I don't love you, David. Not anymore. Just go. Take your money and go to South America."

"No, you have to come with me. You're the only person I've ever cared about, the only one I've ever loved."

"If you ever loved me, you loved me the wrong way," I sobbed. "I don't know how I could have been so blind."

"Don't say that!" he yelled. Then he grabbed my arm, pulling me to my feet. "You're coming with me!"

"No! Let go of me, David. Let go of me!"

"It's Dirk!" he roared, his face turning red. "You're having an affair with Dirk."

I stared at him, trembling, as tears ran down my cheeks.

"You whore!" he raged. Then he slapped me hard, making me cry out.

I tried to pull free, but David's fingers dug into my flesh. I was dizzy from the blow. The whole side of my face was numb. Still, I somehow heard a sound in the hallway—the heavy thump of footsteps—and the door flew open.

It was Dirk, soaking wet, his chest heaving from running up the stairs. He stood there for a brief moment, staring at us. Then he said, "Let go of her, David."

David did let go of me, but at the same time he reached for his bag and pulled out a gun. He pointed it at Dirk. "Don't move."

"No!" I screamed.

"Leave her alone," Dirk commanded. "She doesn't want anything to do with you."

"Shut up!" David snapped. "She's my wife. She's coming with me."

Dirk took a step toward us and David extended the gun as if to shoot.

"Don't," I pleaded. "I'll go with you, David. Just don't hurt anyone. Please." I glanced at Dirk, then at my husband. David looked desperate. He was pale and he was shaking, probably with anger. He'd killed twice. He could do it again.

"No, Allison," Dirk challenged. "You can't go with him."

"It'll be all right," I assured him.

"Give me the keys to your car, Dirk," David demanded.

He felt his pocket. "They're in the ignition. I didn't bother taking them out."

David gestured with the gun. "Move into the corner."

Dirk complied. Then, handing me the bag, David took my arm and led me toward the door.

"Don't try to follow us," he said to Dirk, "or she might get hurt."

David closed the door and we went to the stairs. He began mumbling as he dragged me along. I could tell he'd lost it.

Edwina was waiting at the bottom of the staircase. "Oh, no!" she cried when she saw the gun. David ignored her, dragging me toward the front door. "Son," she called to him, "don't do this. David, please!"

He threw the door open and the icy, wet air came swirling in. He pulled me outside, into the storm. "You'll forgive me, Allison, I know you will. It'll be all right."

He dragged me down the stairs. The Jaguar was at the near edge of the parking area, its lights still on. As David opened the passenger door for me, I glanced up at the house and saw Dirk on the porch. David saw him at the same moment.

"You're not going anywhere," Dirk shouted over the howling wind. "I've got the keys." He held them up, dangling them.

David glanced inside the car and saw they weren't in the ignition. "You bastard!" he bellowed. "You rotten, illegitimate bastard!" Then he pointed the gun at Dirk and fired.

I watched in horror as Dirk slumped down. But then his head popped up over the railing. "It's no use, David," he yelled.

David went berserk. He fired again and again, with the same result. I was in such a daze that it took me a moment to realize what was happening. Dirk was distracting David so I could escape.

I was nearly catatonic with fright, but I pulled myself together enough to back away. Once I got to the rear of the car I turned and began running around the house. But David noticed and started after me.

I plunged into the woods, running blindly. I could hear David behind me. There was barely enough light to see the trees, and the rain continued to pound down. My sweater was completely soaked, my hair plastered to my head. I was slipping and sliding on the muddy ground, falling once and scrambling to my feet, only to fall again a few steps farther on.

But David wasn't having an easy time of it, either. I could hear him cursing in the darkness behind me. He was close enough that I couldn't stop and hide. I had to keep moving.

My heart thundered. Branches from the undergrowth tore at my face and clothes. But I was so terrified I kept going, the cold air beginning to burn my lungs.

When I came out of the woods and into the teeth of the gale, with nothing before me but endless darkness and the terrifying roar of the ocean, I realized I'd come to the sea cliff—the spot I'd walked to that first day.

Behind me I could hear David's shouts, his pleading. I edged out on the rock, hoping to find a crevice I could crawl into, a bush I could slip behind. The rain pelted my body, practically blinding me. The waves were crashing against the rocks with such force that the spray rose more than halfway up the cliff. I could see ghostly white mists below me, but no place to hide.

"Allison!" David shrieked. I spun around. He was about twenty feet away, his sports bag still in his hand.

"Leave me alone!" I screamed, trying to raise my voice above the tumult.

He edged toward me, his hand extended. "Come with me," he begged. "You're my wife. Come with me." He continued to creep toward me. I froze, unable to move forward or back.

It was then I saw Dirk emerge from the woods. He stopped suddenly, seeing David and me perched on the edge of the cliff.

"Dirk!" I cried out.

David spun around, startled. But he must have stepped on a loose rock because his feet went out from under him. I reached toward him, but I couldn't get a grip on the slippery fabric of his Windbreaker. Soundlessly, his bag still in his hand, David dropped from sight.

I peered down at the blackened sea. I think only the wind held me, kept me from falling after him. The next thing I knew, Dirk was jerking me back from the precipice.

My knees buckled. Dirk picked me up in his arms and held me. I began sobbing.

"David fell. I tried . . ."

"I know. There was nothing you could do. He was crazy, Allison. He cracked up."

For a long time Dirk just stood there, holding me. The raging storm no longer mattered. The rain, the wind, the sea. Nothing could harm us now. Not the nebulous past, or even an uncertain future.

Epilogue

IT TOOK ME A LONG TIME to recover from the horror of that night. The events sometimes come back to haunt me in my dreams. But a new life began for me then—my life with Dirk—even as my old life was finally put to rest.

I will never fully understand the man I'd been married to for those brief months. I still grieve for him and for his mother. Edwina died a few days later, despite Dirk's and my efforts to rally her spirits. She was probably the greatest victim of all.

She was buried in the family plot with her husband and her sister, Dirk's mother, Sarah. We visit Arcata at least once a year to remember them with flowers.

Ironically, David's body was never found, though this time there were two witnesses to his death. We erected a monument in his memory because David was a part of the past that brought Dirk and me together, even though he was the dark side of my incredible story.

Dirk and I married three months later and spent two whole weeks in Tahiti on our honeymoon. Dirk loved the northern coast, but we wanted a fresh start. We sold Granville Lumber and bought a ranch on the Central California coast near San Luis Obispo. Like Arcata, it's a college town—small, pleasant, and the sun shines a lot.

We have a son who is three and a daughter who is one. Dirk raises horses. I paint in my studio in our mountain home. I've had exhibitions in San Francisco and Los Angeles.

Gloria and her husband, the architect, come to visit two or three times a year. She never misses a chance to tell me how much I've changed.

Occasionally I do some design work for Gloria—if it's a very important job and she desperately needs my help. But I draw the line at meeting with clients. She laughs when I tell her I can't afford any more adventures. Two husbands are all I ever intend to have, because I really love the one I've got.

A Note from Janice Kaiser

A little over a year ago I complained to Sherie Posesorski, my editor and friend, that I wanted a new challenge. "Why not write a Gothic," she said. "You already love to do mysteries."

"But Gothics are always in the first person," I hedged. "I've never written a book in the first person before."

"Well, you said you wanted a challenge...."

And that is how *Betrayal* was born. From the first sentence, I was hooked. I found it was so much easier to get inside my heroine's head—to make her struggle my struggle, to bring out all the emotion in the story. I discovered I *loved* writing in the first person.

A few months later I told Sherie I wanted to do another book in the first person, this time a detective story. "Sure," she said. "I'd love to see it."

So I wrote that book, *Deceptions,* and when I was finished I called her again. "You know, I'm really hooked on this first-person thing," I said, "but after two of them in a row I think I ought to try something new, another challenge."

And she said to me, "How about an adventure story?"

"An adventure story," I said. "I've never written an adventure story."

"Well, you said you wanted a challenge...."

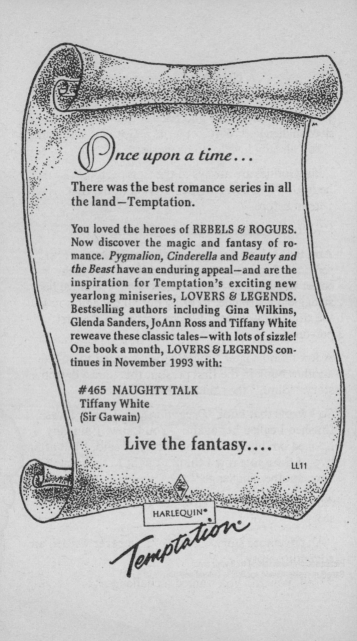

MEN MADE IN AMERICA

Fifty red-blooded, white-hot, true-blue hunks
from every State in the Union!

Look for MEN MADE IN AMERICA! Written by some
of our most poplar authors, these stories feature fifty of
the strongest, sexiest men, each from a different state in
the union!

Two titles available every other month at your favorite
retail outlet.

In November, look for:

STRAIGHT FROM THE HEART by Barbara Delinsky
(Connecticut)
AUTHOR'S CHOICE by Elizabeth August (Delaware)

In January, look for:

DREAM COME TRUE by Ann Major (Florida)
WAY OF THE WILLOW by Linda Shaw (Georgia)

You won't be able to resist MEN MADE IN AMERICA!

LIGHTS, CAMERA, ACTION!

Hollywood Dynasty

HARLEQUIN™ *Temptation*

The Kingstons are Hollywood—two generations of box-office legends in front of and behind the cameras. In this fast-paced world egos compete for the spotlight and intimate secrets make tabloid headlines. Gage—the cinematographer, Pierce—the actor and Claire—the producer struggle for success in an unpredictable business where a single film can make or break you.

By the time the credits roll, will they discover that the ultimate challenge is far more personal? Share the behind-the-scenes dreams and dramas in this blockbuster miniseries by Candace Schuler!

THE OTHER WOMAN, #451 (July 1993)
JUST ANOTHER PRETTY FACE, #459 (September 1993)
THE RIGHT DIRECTION, #467 (November 1993)

Coming soon to your favorite retail outlet.

HARLEQUIN®

Temptation®

FIRST-PERSON PERSONAL

Nothing is more intimate than first-person personal narration....

Two emotionally intense, intimate romances told in first person, in the tradition of Daphne du Maurier's *Rebecca* from bestselling author Janice Kaiser.

Recently widowed Allison Stephens travels to her husband's home to discover the truth about his death and finds herself caught up in a web of family secrets and betrayals. Even more dangerous is the passion ignited in her by the man her husband hated most—Dirk Granville.
BETRAYAL, Temptation #462, October 1993

P.I. Darcy Hunter is drawn into the life of Kyle Weston, the man who had been engaged to her deceased sister. Seeing him again sparks long-buried feelings of love and guilt. Working closely together on a case, their attraction escalates. But Darcy fears it is memories of her sister that Kyle is falling in love with.
DECEPTIONS, Temptation #466, November 1993

Each book tells you the heroine's compelling story in her own personal voice. Wherever Harlequin books are sold.

If you enjoyed this book by

JANICE KAISER

Here's your chance to order more stories by one of
Harlequin's favorite authors:

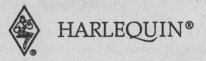

HARLEQUIN®